MURDER
SO STRANGE

MUCKRAKER MYSTERY #2
CLIFTON · NELSON

Murder So Strange (Muckraker Mystery #2)
Ted Clifton & Stanley Nelson
ISBN 978-1-77342-030-1

Produced by IndieBookLauncher.com
www.IndieBookLauncher.com
Editing: Nassau Hedron
Cover Design: Saul Bottcher
Interior Design and Typesetting: Saul Bottcher

The body text of this book is set in Adobe Caslon.

Also Available
E-book edition, ISBN 978-1-77342-031-8

CONTENTS

1

LOW TIMES IN HIGH PLACES

1969. Neil Armstrong becomes the first human to set foot on the moon. The average new car sets you back about $3,200—of course, with the average American income at $8,500, that's a bundle. Richard Nixon has been sworn in as the thirty-seventh president of the United States. Secret negotiations have failed to end the Vietnam War, and violent protests are growing.

Flashing emergency lights outside a stately mansion in the Nichols Hills enclave of Oklahoma City drew little attention. The blinking lights and other activity were unusual and very visible, but neighbors in this exclusive area of town weren't nosy, or at least didn't let themselves appear that way, and they were generally not close to their fellow residents, physically or otherwise. Even so, United States Senator Bruce Knight and his wife, who had owned a home in the neighborhood for more than twenty years, might have been the first to complain about all the activity, had it not been on *their* own doorstep.

Since becoming a senator, Knight had principally lived in Washington. The gossip among the cloistered neighbors was that Mrs. Knight never adapted to life in D.C. and preferred her Oklahoma City house, with or without the senator.

The latest police car to pull up discharged Sergeant Maxwell Stevens onto the Knight's massive circular driveway. He turned to a patrolman slouching against another car. "Whadda we got?"

"A medical emergency. Live-in nurse called 911. Ambulance arrived about the same time I got here. They've been in and out with equipment and stuff. The last guy who came out said the lady was dead. His guess was some kind of drug overdose."

Stevens flinched. "You sayin' Senator Knight's wife died?"

"Yeah. She was the only one in the house, other than two servants and the nurse."

"Jeez. I better call the chief and let him know. This means we're going to have a whole herd of nosy reporters all over this place." Stevens got on the radio. "Need to talk to the chief. We've got a situation out here in his neighborhood that I'm sure he'll want to know about." That, along with what he'd found out so far, was relayed to the chief's top assistant, an attractive young woman named Jackie Carter. The exact nature of Jackie's relationship with Chief Underwood was the subject of more rumors than just about anything else in town, even who would be starting quarterback for the Sooners. Carter said she'd let the chief know and that Stevens should secure the area and "keep the asshole reporters as far away as possible."

The early February evening had a typical bad-weather-month chill. Stevens grabbed his jacket and headed for the well-lit house. Other police and medical vehicles pulled up. Soon the expected herd of reporters gathered, prompted by their sources. Some of the more inventive ones were able to monitor police band radio.

By far the most disruptive were the TV reporters. Their

equipment and attitudes were so intrusive even the genteel neighbors could not ignore their arrival. Before the police had much of a barrier set up, a crowd of well-to-do rubberneckers blossomed, gossiping about their neighborhood drama.

"Hey, Tommy, did I wake you up?"

"Nah, not really. What's goin' on?" Tommy Jacks, the *OK Journal's* top political reporter and columnist, was a notorious nap-taker and not thrilled about the ribbing he took for that. But the caller was June Newton, his overworked and underappreciated assistant city editor, so he had to play nice.

"Got a hot lead. Big police presence with ambulances at Senator Knight's mansion in Nichols Hills. Word is the senator's wife, Janet, is dead. Expecting some kind of news conference at the house since every TV station in town is there—hard for the police chief to ignore that. Plus, strange as it may seem, he happens to live out there. How the hell he can afford it is a story we should check on at some point. Anyway, if you can get over there, might be something you could work into your column. Bound to be some political angle. Plus, rumors about Knight's womanizing are always worth looking into. Vince is already headed out there." Vince was Vince Young, a top *Journal* reporter and a friend of Tommy's.

"Okay. Give me an address."

Tommy Jacks had been in the middle of a personal whirlwind for what felt like years but had actually only been a few months. He'd graduated from the University of Oklahoma with a degree in journalism then almost immediately became a stringer for the *Journal*. It was the absolute ground floor for reporting—maybe even the basement —but at least he'd been assigned to cover the state capitol. With hard work, and some serious connections in state politics and the *Journal's* ownership, he quickly became a political columnist.

Along with Tommy's newfound fame came tragedy. His girlfriend was killed in a confrontation with the Capitol Police. Judy Jackson had become his first true love and his greatest loss. He had to relearn each day how to deal with soul-crushing sadness.

Still far from the Knight residence, Tommy caught sight of emergency lights and vehicles clogging the street—a circus atmosphere surrounding a tragic death. It was at times like this when Tommy wondered about the profession he'd chosen. The bright lights of the TV crews were trained on attractive men and women who delivered heartfelt statements about what they imagined might have happened inside the house behind them, only as a means to sell advertisements for car dealerships, beauty-care products, and furniture stores. It wasn't nearly as noble as the ideal Tommy was taught in journalism school.

"Hey, Tommy. Welcome to the show." Vince Young joked, as if he was just an observer rather than a participant.

"Yeah, quite an event." Tommy felt a growing excitement with all the activity, but it seemed unprofessional to show it. "I thought she died of natural causes. Why all the police? Looks more like a murder scene."

"Good question. Don't know. All I've heard is that she was alone in the house with a couple of staff people and her nurse, and she had some kind of bad reaction to her medicine. Someone called an ambulance, but she died not long after they got here. Maybe the police are here just to keep us at arm's length.

Unless, of course, what we've been told is just a bunch of lies—*though I can't imagine that*." Vince rolled his eyes.

"Well, something doesn't smell right. June said the police chief lives in this neighborhood. How can a cop afford this kind of luxury—even the top one?"

"You're just full of good questions. The most likely answer is that he's on the take. Now, *he says* he inherited money from some distant relative. He sure doesn't try to hide it, so maybe he did."

"Hello, handsome." Tommy blushed. He knew that voice. Tracy Clark, one of the beautiful TV people pretending to be reporters, appeared. She was also—far more importantly—his self-selected, unofficially adopted mom.

He grinned. "Hello, beautiful." He gave her a quick hug and introduced Vince Young. Vince was older and more sophisticated than Tommy—at least, according to Vince himself—but he seemed in awe of Tracy. He stammered out a "hello," but mostly just stared.

Very mature, Tommy thought, but rather than remark on Vince, he asked Tracy, "What do you think's going to happen?"

"Nobody seems to know. Very strange, this being a natural death, to have all these police, even if it is the wife of our all-powerful senator." She wrinkled her nose like she'd caught scent of something foul. "Our news manager's convinced that there's been some sort of crime and figures that's why there's been so much delay. They needed time to allow all these top dogs to show up. We broke into our regular broadcast about twenty minutes ago with a bulletin about it. It seemed premature to me, but he insisted because Channel 8's already done one. I think they'll have some hostile reporters on their hands if they just come out and say, 'Yeah, she's dead,' and don't give us more than that."

Tommy, still a novice, was amazed by the competitive nature of the news-gathering beast. The two major daily newspapers in Oklahoma City attacked each other with unfettered bitterness almost every day. The TV people had their own war, even if they would, on occasion, take up arms against the newspapers based on the most trivial negative comment any paper made about a TV report. There were no allies—only potential enemies. The competitive juices flowed from one feud to another, and along the way the public was informed of matters great and small. For those on the inside, this verbal battle superseded whatever was covered. It was all about winning. This evening's events were a prime example.

"Guess I'd better get back in front of the lights. Looks like they're getting ready for another live shot." Tracy gave Tommy a motherly look. "You need to come by and see your dad, Tommy. I know you think he's fine not seeing you, but it's not true. He worries about you all the time. Plus, he's still a built-in source for all of the political history you could ever want about this town. You be good—come by and see us, okay?"

Tommy nodded and gave her another careful hug—he didn't want to mess up her hair or makeup.

"Wow," Vince blurted out at last, "are you related to Tracy Clark?"

"No, not exactly. She's dating my dad. Well, actually they're living together." Tommy paused. "She's been about the best friend I ever had. Without her, I'm not sure I'd be here today."

"Hey," Vince said, "looks like we're getting some action. See ya." He headed out to get a front-row spot. Vince worked on deadlines and dealt with hard news. Tommy wasn't subject to the same demands as a columnist, so he settled for the back row.

"Thank you all for being here," Deputy Police Chief Tom Lawson began. "We're going to keep this short, no matter how much you shout. This is a residential neighborhood, and we're going to clear everyone out in just a few minutes. Chief Underwood will make a brief statement, and then he'll take a few questions. I expect we'll have more information in the morning, and, if necessary, we'll hold another news conference tomorrow, downtown. Chief?"

The chief stepped forward, looking regal with his six-foot-two frame and full head of snow-white hair, just right for a crown. He wore his full dress uniform for the occasion, with its assortment of ribbons and awards, and his non-standard issue six-shooter. He was a show all on his own. "About two hours ago, Janet Knight, the beloved wife of Senator Bruce Knight, passed away. I've known the senator and his wife for many years, and this is a great personal loss. I've been in touch with the senator, who, at this time, is en route from Washington, D.C. All arrangements and any announcement regarding services for Mrs. Knight will be made through the senator's office. At this time, we're unable to release any information regarding the cause of Mrs. Knight's passing. There is no suspicion of foul play. The medical examiner, however, has not been able to determine the exact cause of death, so that will require further investigation. The examiner has assured me personally that this process will be carried out as quickly as possible and with great care, and he'll be able to conclusively determine the exact cause of death in very short order. Once again, let me be clear: there is no reason to think that anything happened other than Janet Knight passed away after a long illness due to natural causes. Questions? Yes, Vince."

"Chief, we've heard some say Mrs. Knight was on medication, and she suffered a severe reaction which might have been the cause of her death. Is there anything to that?"

"Vince, I don't know where you people get this stuff. Seems to me you talk to each other and just make it up. I've already told you we don't know the cause of death, and I'm not going to speculate. I'll let the medical examiner do his job, and once I have his report, we'll tell you what we know. That's all the questions. You'll need to clear out of this area at once."

Underwood, known for his disdain toward the press, walked away, followed by a subtle flurry of boos. Like it or not, the news conference was over. Shoving and prodding by police made clear it was time to leave the Knight estate. Tommy looked for Vince but couldn't find him. He caught sight of ambulance attendants wheeling out a gurney bearing what presumably was the body of the late Mrs. Knight. Other eagle-eyed journalists saw it, too. There was a brief frenzy of picture-taking.

Tommy achieved local fame writing for one of the two newspapers in town, although he knew one of the reasons he had his job was his willingness to work for paltry wages. Also, he had few other job options. The *Journal* was in the midst of financial calamity, having trouble meeting obligations, even if its owner was one of the richest men in the state. Bill Anderson had made it clear he'd invested all he was willing to part with, and the paper had to make it on its own. That meant poor pay with no hope of a raise in the immediate future. It didn't make for a happy newsroom. Tommy, however, was pleased to have a job. By necessity and habit he was living cheap and didn't need much money. He found his dilapidated 1955 Ford Fairlane, unlocked and unharmed, right where he'd left it. It was a heap, but it was paid for and not likely to be stolen. He headed to his apartment in one of the worst sections of town. It wasn't much but it was his.

When he got there, the phone was ringing. "Hello."

"Tommy, it's June again. Look, I just got a call from Chuck, the police beat guy. He said Taylor Albright's been arrested. He's being held downtown. I didn't know who to call other than you—guess I don't have your dad's number anymore. Just thought someone should go and see if they can bail him out."

"Do you know why?"

"He was arrested at Triple's. The charge seems to be drunk and disorderly."

Shit, Tommy thought. "I'll see what I can find out." Albright was the smartest and most difficult person Tommy knew—and his mentor. He owed him a great deal. And this didn't sound like him.

2

JAIL BREAK

Tommy's experience at extracting people from jail was exactly zero, nil, *nada*. He called Joe Louongo, the less-than-reputable attorney who had a long relationship with Albright and Tommy's dad, but the lawyer didn't answer—typical for him. After a full day of doing what other people told him to do, he was beat. With reluctance he got into his car and headed downtown to the police station.

Tommy entered the impressive lobby and found a window marked "Information," where he asked about the arrest of Taylor Albright. The officer behind the window grunted, perhaps to indicate he at least understood the question. He shuffled paper. He went to the back of the room and made a phone call. "No booking for a Taylor Albright. Are you sure he was arrested today?" The officer sounded bored.

"Yeah, that's what I was told. Look, I'm a newspaper reporter and my editor said he'd been arrested."

"Reporter? Shit. Why didn't you say you're a reporter?" The man was suddenly acting as if he was under siege.

"I'm not here as a reporter. He's my friend." Tommy's voice got a bit louder than he meant it to—the officer's reaction had caught him off guard.

"You gonna start making trouble? I'll call the duty officers."

The clerkish cop grabbed the phone.

Tommy was confused and more than a little scared. Could he actually be arrested at a police station for asking a question at the information window? "Hey, I'm not causing trouble. I just want information. Besides, isn't it a matter of public record who you have locked up?"

Too late.

"Stand back from the window, now!" shouted one of two officers entering the lobby a couple of doors down from the window. His gun was drawn and pointed at Tommy.

Flashbacks struck him, of police at the state capitol, guns, and Judy dying. "Don't shoot! Leave me alone, don't shoot!" he shouted wildly, reeling backward, falling.

Then another voice began hollering, much louder than any-one else's. "What the fuck is happening here! You goddamn cops better put your guns away! He's a reporter, and I'm his attorney, and we will sue your fuckin' asses off!" Joe Louongo had been found, and definitely heard.

The police looked stunned and angry. They seemed to rec-ognize Louongo. And while their fellow cops might consider them heroes if they shot the annoying mouthpiece, it would cause far more trouble than it was worth. They holstered their guns and called for medical staff. Tommy had cut his head on one of the metal benches and sat on the floor, mumbling to himself.

"Tommy, it's Louongo. Are you okay?" Louongo switched from nervous to angry and then back again. "These goddamn cops are in big fuckin' trouble. You're going to be fine, though." He glowered at the officers.

Tommy blinked several times and seemed to come out of

his daze. He looked up at Louongo. "Where the hell have you been? I need help."

Louongo smiled. "Nosy reporter, always asking questions. Yeah, kid, I know you need help. That's why I'm here. Albright got his one phone call, and it was to me. He asked me to call the paper because it seems they'd been calling and raising hell about him being arrested. Anyway, I called the *Journal* and some lady told me she'd asked you to come down here and get him out. Sonofabitch, kid, you don't know how to do this shit. This is what I do—why didn't you call me?"

"I did call you. You never answer your damn phone." Tommy felt okay, though a little embarrassed. A nurse appeared, and without so much as an introduction, began dressing the wound on his head. With practiced efficiency, she had it cleaned and bandaged in a matter of minutes. Without a word, she left; duty done.

In the meantime, the cops spoke with the jumpy officer from the information window. Tommy could hear they were furious with him.

The spokesman for their group came over. "Sorry about that." His manner seemed genuinely contrite. "Looks like our guy over there may have overreacted and reported something that wasn't really accurate. Sorry for the misunderstanding." They all had the good manners to look embarrassed.

Tommy looked up and smiled, just wanting this to be over. "It's okay. Maybe I shouldn't have raised my voice. No harm."

"No harm, my ass," Louongo put in. "You can't storm in here with guns drawn on a citizen who hasn't done anything but ask a question at the *goddamn motherfucking information window*. This isn't Gestapo headquarters, for Christ's sake. My client may be generous enough to want to forgive and forget, but that's not who I am. This is not over, got it?" Louongo put on a show worthy of a larger audience, which was hardly unusual for him. And the two cops were definitely getting the message—they damn near bowed while they exited the lobby.

Soon, new people appeared to discuss the situation with Louongo. One, Captain Someone-or-other, seemed quite apologetic. He also said Albright would be released at once without having to post bail. Louongo, being Louongo, gave no ground. The more the captain humiliated himself, the more Louongo demanded.

"I think we need to get Taylor and get out of here, okay?" Tommy, the clearest victim in the whole mess, wanted it to be over. It was past his bedtime, and while he appreciated what Louongo had done, he was getting tired of hearing his voice.

Soon, Taylor Albright appeared. He didn't look like he'd been drunk. He was always disorderly, at least in his appearance. But as far as Tommy knew, that wasn't a crime.

"Hey, thanks, both of you. Sure didn't mean to cause all this trouble." Albright seemed upset. "Tommy, you ought to head home. You look like shit."

Tommy smiled, but bit his tongue. *Compared to you, I look great.* "Yeah, it's been a rough day. What happened to you?"

Albright held up his hand. "Not tonight. Meet me at Denny's tomorrow morning—say around nine, not my normal six. I'll explain everything. But for now, I think we all need some rest. Louongo, how about a ride?"

They walked out into the cold night and said their goodbyes. Tommy headed toward his car, hoping for a quick trip home. He was young, but even so, he was getting close to exhaustion.

And he needed time to think about his spontaneous reaction to the police yelling and pointing guns at him. It scared him that he'd lost control so quickly and easily.

Denny's, on Classen Boulevard, was the place where Albright almost always began his day. He didn't drive—didn't know how. Being from New York, he was most comfortable in a cab, on the subway, or on a city bus. Since coming to Oklahoma to help a friend campaign for governor, he'd discovered the norm here was to own a car or two. There was no subway, cab service was spotty, and the city bus service was underfunded, catering mostly to those less fortunate with little political clout. He complained, but he also adapted. He was a notorious ride moocher. His daily routine was to secure an armload of morning papers, both local and national, from a newsstand near his home, then trek to Denny's for breakfast and a lot of reading.

Tommy got to Denny's a few minutes before nine. Albright wasn't there. Knowing the man's habits, Tommy wasn't worried. He took a seat at the counter, ordered a coffee, and waited. It was almost nine-thirty when Albright finally arrived, looking frazzled, arms loaded with papers, clearly angry. He and Tommy got a booth.

"Damned bus service here is completely useless. The bus broke down, and it took forever for them to get a new one out to pick us up. Just absurd. I may write a whole edition of *The Banner* about nothing but the lousy services in this cowtown." Letting off steam seemed to improve Albright's attitude. *The Banner* was a tabloid by which he spread political gossip, published with the generous support of a local printer. It came out according to his whim and need, and when the printer could afford a little free press time. It was a favorite with journalists, who fed Albright stories their organizations wouldn't print or air, but wasn't much read beyond that. Nothing seemed to intimidate Albright. He couldn't be sued successfully since most of his substantial assets were buried in an untouchable trust established by his long-suffering family. He was judgment-proof in an industry where it was already very difficult to sue. *The Banner* was aggressive and loud, but had a tiny audience.

Tommy was familiar with Albright's unusual personality and knew it was best to wait before bringing up the reason he'd come, at least until Albright had his breakfast and scanned most of the papers scattered all over the table. Tommy found the front page of the *Journal* and read Vince's story about the previous night's event at the Knight mansion.

"What do you know about Senator Knight?"

"Most of what I know is pure gossip. Your father's the one to ask. He's had dealings with the man and doesn't have much good to say about him. The no-can-print version is that he's a complete jerk. Moved to Washington and never came back. Sent his wife back to Oklahoma so he could have free reign to chase women, although there's a particularly ugly story that says he also chases men."

Ask a gossip monger for gossip, and what do you get? "I hadn't thought about the senator being a Democrat. I'll ask my dad about him, then. Do you know why his wife was ill?"

"The only thing I know for sure is that she's rarely been seen outside the house for the past few years. The word on the street was that she'd become a drug addict. Of course, at her station in life, that means prescription drugs. Her doctor's

Ralph Jenkins, who's known as the biggest drug pusher in the state. I had some good quality dirt on her and the doctor, but I never used it—even *The Banner* has standards, low as they may be." Albright was giving Tommy the eye, as if to suggest he was about through with the subject.

"Okay. So now tell me why you were arrested at Triple's. Were you drunk and disorderly?" Tommy spat it out a little harshly, but he was frustrated. Why did every conversation with his friend and mentor have to be so difficult?

"First, none of this goes into the paper. Got it?" After Tommy nodded, he went on, "I was arrested on a false charge after a little altercation caused by a real asshole—Dealin' Dave. Ever heard of him?"

Tommy grinned, puzzled. "The car dealer, you mean? With those corny ads on TV?"

"That's him. In the last two issues of *The Banner* I had a small article including rumors going around about his new business venture—prostitution. His first response was to threaten to sue me. I said, 'Bring it on, asshole.' His next idea was to threaten to hurt me. And, guess what? I said, 'Bring it on, asshole.' So, he did."

Tommy couldn't help it—he started laughing. This was so Albright as to be classic. He knew no fear. Where a normal person backed away, he charged in headfirst. "What actually happened?"

"Dealin' Dave—his real name's David Harris—came into Triple's with a couple of goons. He seemed to know I was going to be there, or maybe they'd been following me, I don't know. But they came up to me, and Harris tells me if I don't stop printing stories about him, he'll have me killed. Well,

I said some wiseass thing to him, and his two goons started roughing me up some and poured whiskey on me. Harris leans over and lights a match and says some idiotic thing about setting me on fire. The cops show up somewhere around then and arrested *me*. I have no explanation for that other than that they were working with Harris. I think the whole point of this was just to scare me—and it worked."

"My god, Taylor. This guy's a loudmouth car dealer on late night TV. Is he really into prostitution?" Now Tommy was afraid for him.

"Well, remember this is just stuff I hear. Who knows what's real and what's just made-up crap? It seems that one of your dad's old friends, Big Frank Martin, left the country. That's created a huge vacuum in the realm of illegal activities. Harris's little brother—you're not going to believe this, but he goes by 'Little Dave,' I'm not kidding—decided to move in and take over the prostitution business. Why his big brother got involved is a little murky, but could be as simple as it's easy money, and he's helping his little brother. Anyway, they bought some motels. One downtown, one on Tenth, and one on Reno west of downtown. Those are the basis of their new business, with a lot of less-than-pure women, of course. Convenient locations all over town. Sounds like Dealin' Dave, doesn't it?"

"Why in the hell would you print this stuff? You could get killed."

Albright shrugged. "Not sure why I did. Beginning to think it might've been a mistake."

"What are you going to do to protect yourself?"

Albright winked. "My bodyguards are returning." He smiled his trademark smile, smug and annoying.

OK Journal

My View—Tommy Jacks

Police and ambulance vehicles rushed to a home in Nichols Hills last night, alerted by a caller who said a woman, presumably Janet Knight, the wife of U.S. Sen. Bruce Knight, D-Okla., needed help. Depending on which source you believe, she was either passing away or already gone. Maybe.

Chief Walter Underwood, he of imperious bearing and a finely polished Colt Peacemaker in a holster that looks like it was stolen from Roy Rogers, stepped forth to tell the press that Mrs. Knight had died, placing the time at just about when the ambulance showed up, give or take a half-hour.

As complicated as that seemed, things got worse. Our man Vince Young asked whether Mrs. Knight might have had a reaction to medication—not whether she *did*, just whether she might have—and Underwood

took that as the cue to break into one of his favorite songs. You know—the one about how we reporters make stuff up. And no, he didn't actually answer the question.

While we're on the subject of Chief Walter Underwood's police department, let's take a moment to offer some helpful tips. The ones I have in mind are especially good for anyone who happens to be unfortunate enough to have to deal with Underwood or the department.

This isn't for the benefit of the criminal element. They're on their own. This advice is for the average, innocent citizen of our fair town who wants to, say, ask for information.

At police headquarters, there's actually a place for that. It's a window in the great big lobby, like the kind ticket clerks and bank tellers work behind. It says

"Information," in big letters right above it. You can't miss it.

But here's the tip. At that window, don't so much as mention newspaper reporters, or probably even television or radio reporters. Heck, if you're even carrying a newspaper or radio, lose it somewhere before you get to that window. I'm serious. Bad things can happen if you don't.

I speak from experience. If only I could remember anything I'd done to make the cop in the information booth feel so out of sorts that he deemed it necessary to call two more officers to the scene as if I'd threatened him. Which I didn't, unless asking a simple question is a threat in your book. And on top of that, it's hard to understand why at least one of those two who came to his rescue considered it necessary to draw his service revolver and

point it at me.

The apparent transgression that led to that response was, so far as can be determined, twofold:

1. The "Information" officer was asked a question.

2. The citizen asking the question mentioned he was a reporter (although I did specify I was off duty).

Apart from that, it's a bit tough to figure why I found myself looking down a .38 caliber barrel.

To the credit of the officers involved, not only did they not shoot me—as much as that may disappoint some people—they later seemed to understand their actions didn't fit the situation.

I'm not that interested in punitive action. I just want to know why this happened. Maybe Chief Underwood might know. 🍒

3

LONG AGO CONNECTIONS

1922. It was a year of unlimited optimism. Everyone was going to get rich. The first radio was introduced into the White House by President Warren G. Harding. Oil was king in Oklahoma. Wildcatters were striking it rich one week and pouring their money into dry holes the next. J.H. Gilmore, the publisher of the *Oklahoma Sun,* was one of the richest men in the state. An early supporter of the "high school movement," Gilmore and his paper were a major factor in a dramatic increase in the number of free schools, especially high schools, available to all students—almost. It was a white-only advantage, but it included most economic classes. Central High School in Oklahoma City was one of the largest in the state and highly regarded for its excellent academics and state champion football team.

CENTRAL HIGH SCHOOL, OKLAHOMA CITY, OKLAHOMA

School was over for the day, and the usual group was hanging around outside. Some puffed cigarettes, taking care that no grownups saw them. Three stood apart, just talking.

"I hate school. All this crap about a better future, it's just nonsense. I'll make my own future in football. Or maybe with these." Frank Martin held up his fists so everyone would be clear about what he meant. He was the star fullback for the state champion Central High Cardinals. Few people thought you could make a living playing football, but Frank was surely mean enough to do it with his fists, one way or another.

Ralph Jenkins smirked. "I think you're right, Frank. Either beat people up, or have someone beat you up—that ought to be a great future. As for me, I'm gonna let my old man support me until the old bastard dies. Then I'll live like a king off his fortune."

Bruce Knight chuckled. "You know, Ralph—I bet your old man is planning on spending all that money just before he dies, leaving you with zippo." Bruce was class president and an over-achiever. Everyone, except Bruce, thought he was going to be successful and that he didn't belong with the other two. He was considered college material and with a degree would be some kind of leader. Plus, Knight's family had money. They were not super-rich like the oil people, but his family owned much of the farmland that thriving Oklahoma City was in the process of chewing up with its unheard-of growth. The Knights were newly wealthy and notably recent snobs.

"Yeah, you might be right, Brucey. I might fool him, though—just shoot the old fart one day." No one laughed. Ralph made almost everyone nervous. He was the smartest kid in school. His teachers described him as brilliant, maybe even a genius. But just being around Ralph Jenkins made people instinctively uneasy and a jumpy.

The three lived on the same block, not far from the school, and were sort of friends; mostly the result of their families living in close proximity. The Knights had announced to everyone in the neighborhood they would be moving as soon as the school year was over, shamelessly bragging they were going to Crown Heights, many steps up the economic ladder.

Bruce arrived home to find no one there. His parents had been doing virtually nothing for months besides energetically spending money made from selling off farmland his father inherited. Neither were farm people; their only connection to the land was the price it could bring. Bruce thought they were making a mistake. There was no way he could have said anything about it to his dad without getting a sharp blow to the head, so he tried to talk to his mother, who simply said, "You only live once." Factually true, but you could easily outlive your money at the rate they were spending. Bruce knew if he were in charge, he would have kept most of the land since he thought real estate was the best investment. But then they couldn't spend like there was no tomorrow.

In an impressive act that seemed like kindness, but was likely a ploy to get him out of their hair, they gave him a very large sum of money to attend his college of choice back east—Yale. He knew his parents thought spending so much money on college was a waste, and he was certain it was the last money he'd see from them.

Oklahomans seemed genuine and kind enough, but in some fundamental way, he knew he was different. That wasn't bad in itself—just lonely. Going to Yale was more than a way to get a good education and gain contacts for his future—it was a way to go somewhere different, where he might feel more at home.

Even Yale's city sounded so foreign: New Haven, Connecticut. He desperately wanted to be there now. No more walks to and from school with Ralph and Frank, each frightening in his own way. Bruce didn't know what he wanted to be or do, but he was sure he was going to be happiest somewhere other than Oklahoma.

Ralph Jenkins's old man once said the damned kid was born mad as hell. He wasn't a healthy baby—almost died—and he cried a lot. His father was a mean drunk who thought family was all about having people to hurt. He didn't work but always seemed to be in the dough. Ralph figured it was something illegal and maybe he didn't want to know.

Going to high school was a way for Ralph to show off his main asset, which was his mind. He knew he was smarter than anyone at his school, maybe smarter than anyone in the whole damned state. College was only for rich kids, but it still was what Ralph wanted. He'd never discussed it with anyone, especially his dad, but he wanted to go to medical school. During his early years, he'd spent more time with doctors than with his parents. One in particular did more than anyone else to keep him alive. Ralph was a baby at the time, though, so he hadn't known anything about it until he met the man later. Doctor Hawthorn was everything his parents were not. He talked to Ralph like a real person, not just a kid, and told Ralph to visit him anytime.

Ralph started doing just that. Doctor Hawthorn became Ralph's ideal of what a person should be. Because of him, Ralph wanted to be a doctor, even after a visit in the last year of the doctor's life when Ralph asked him if he thought he would make a good doctor.

"Ralph, you're very smart. Medical school would be relatively easy for you. And you've become one of my greatest friends. So, I hate saying this to you, but—it's going to be difficult being a doctor as long as you hate so much. You have to let the hate go and love your fellow man if you want to be a good doctor." Ralph could see the sadness in his eyes.

Ralph never went back. Not long after, Hawthorn died. Ralph had decided to keep his hate. And now it grew.

Several prestigious schools offered him scholarships. He'd been a straight-A student at Central and received recommendations from his teachers, although none said anything personal about Ralph, and they definitely didn't mention how he scared them. One school asked Ralph to visit the campus to take a new IQ test. The results were the highest anyone there had ever seen. They offered him a full scholarship to enter their medical school. The dean thought Ralph Jenkins might someday make his institution famous.

The Martin home was chaotic, constantly full of relatives who needed a roof over their heads. And Frank's dad was too weak-willed to tell the freeloaders to get lost. Frank would have taken care of them right quick, and none would have dared challenge him.

His father worked twelve-hour days at a factory that made cheap furniture and dragged himself home to listen to his ungrateful relatives complain about the food, the bedrooms, or any of a thousand other things. He would listen and say he'd see what he could do. Frank hated him for letting people walk all over him. Knock them in the head a little, and they'd straighten up.

Frank worked weekends as a meatpacker in the stockyards, walking blocks to catch a trolley heading there. He'd have worked during the week, too, but his mother wouldn't let him quit school. She didn't want him to be stupid. But that didn't matter to him, as long as he was feared.

The stockyards felt more like home to him than his house. It was run by tough guys, and nobody took shit from anybody. People knew him and treated him with respect. It was his world.

There were only a few weeks left in school, after which he'd work full-time. As soon as he got his first full paycheck, he'd move out. He'd find a little apartment where he could be the boss and not have to watch his father give away hard-earned money to moochers.

Frank never made friends easily. About the only people he'd talked to at school were Bruce and Ralph. He laughed at the thought—he knew he was the odd man out in that group. Both those guys would get great educations, but Frank thought he might end up at least as successful as they would, if not more so, mostly because there were no real limits on what he was willing to do. He would make the world his own, on his terms. He might not know some of the stuff those guys did, but he had a different kind of smarts—the kind that could only come from living in the dirt and not caring. He knew he had an edge about him that made people nervous, even fearful. He would use it to make his fortune.

4

LEGISLATIVE SESSION

The Oklahoma House and Senate meet in legislative session once a year, from January until around May or June, depending on the level of rancor and severity of physical threats—as well as the more mundane consideration of passing bills. Special sessions can be called by the governor, although he's normally very pleased to see all the legislators leave the state capitol as soon as possible.

The legislature was once controlled by Republicans, a situation that came about after a number of Democrats switched parties to protest the election of Raymond Jacks as state party chairman at an unruly state convention. Being a man of the people, Ray immediately clashed with the power behind the conservative turncoats—J.H. Gilmore, the tyrannical owner of a business empire that included the largest newspaper in the state, *The Oklahoma Sun*. After J.H. was hospitalized by a massive heart attack, his mantle was taken up by his son, Robert "Robbie" Gilmore.

Ironically, Robbie and Ray had been childhood friends. Their parents were neighbors until financial calamity claimed the Jacks's wealth. Soon after, the elder Jacks committed suicide. Robbie's family instantly shunned Ray's, and the boys traveled very different paths to adulthood. Eventually they became enemies. Ray's fall from good public standing was engineered by both Gilmores, culminating in a false conviction that put Ray in state prison for many years.

The day Ray was released from prison and reunited with Tommy was one of the best of his life. Prison and time had changed him into a calmer, more thoughtful man. He had endured a lot of pain in his life, the greatest being the loss of his first wife to cancer. She had been Tommy's mother and Ray's first love. Ray regretted his failure at parenting, adding that to his list of sins. The hardship of prison taught him the value of family and soothed some of his bitterness.

After his release, he moved into Tommy's untidy apartment, but it quickly became clear that living together put a strain on their new relationship. Before prison, Ray had also gotten to know Tracy Clark while trying to help her find answers about her father's mysterious death, and she'd visited him at the penitentiary a couple of times. They developed a very real connection, sharing their personal stories, joys and sorrows. It was a bonding that was totally unexpected. She offered Ray her spare bedroom until he could find his own place. Ray insisted their relationship was strictly platonic, but Tommy was skeptical.

Next for Ray was the matter of regaining employment. He'd been state chairman of the Democratic Party for years, a job that seemed to put him at odds with people. One of his few friends was one of the best lawyers in the state, Lawrence J Alexander III, known as "LJ3" in the gossip columns and "Larry" to his friends. Larry did his best work behind the scenes, so coverage on him was limited to the society pages. Every time a socialite got married, or high society gathered, Lawrence Alexander was there. There was no one more liked—or more feared—than LJ3.

Although Ray wasn't begging, he was, frankly, looking for help.

"Ray," Larry admonished him, "I told you years ago that you needed to get out of politics and find honest work."

"Well, that *sounds* good, but most of what I know is politics. Not sure I would be much good at anything else."

"It's a dirty business. Look at all the grief it's caused you. My god, Ray, you just got out of prison because you were so good at politics. Maybe you should look at something a little less threatening." Larry was smiling. He knew, as Ray did, there was only one field where Ray could make himself useful, and that was politics. "The session's about to start, and T.D. McFadden just lost his top assistant. He owes me, and he owes you. If you want that horrible job, I'm sure he'll gladly give it to you. But think about this: you're immediately going to come into contact with all the assholes who turned their backs on you. And you won't be able to punch a single one, or even cuss them out. Are you sure you want to jump into that?"

Ray wasn't sure. But other than politics, just about all he could do was sweep floors. "Yeah, it won't be easy. But I'm sure. Would you call T.D. for me?"

T.D. McFadden was a Democratic representative from Oklahoma County, a fierce fighter for "his people," and in constant conflict with the power elite. He and Ray had once made a formidable team until Ray criticized T.D.'s position on a bill that would have stripped significant funding from rural programs. From this basic disagreement grew a thriving, often personal feud. Ray's downfall occurred before they could mend their differences.

"Sonofabitch, Ray. It's good to see you. That was some bad shit that happened, with you endin' up in prison. I should have done more to prevent that. Seemed like I was wrapped up in my own world and not payin' enough attention."

"Don't worry about it, T.D. I stepped on the Gilmores' toes once too often, and they got me. I'm ready to move on. Appreciate you thinking about me for your assistant job."

"Well, Larry can be kind of pushy." T.D. chuckled, but was giving Ray the eye. "Frankly, Ray, I'm a little unsure. You and I never settled our little disagreement on the rural funding bill. Thought you might still hold a grudge."

"Ancient history. Water under the bridge. And you know I can do a good job for you. Not many people on the street know more about this madhouse than I do." Ray feared he came off to T.D. as a little too desperate—but of course, he was.

"Guess you really need this job." T.D. said. "I do have a concern about all the history you bring. I'm pretty damn good at making enemies, and I sure don't need you bringing in more on your own." T.D. paused. "Still, I also know I wouldn't have this job if it weren't for you. I haven't forgotten how much you helped me, not only to win, but to figure out how to succeed. I owe you a lot. Just don't want to put you in a spot that's bad for both of us."

"I hear you. No question, I still have some enemies—some pretty powerful ones, like Robbie Gilmore—but I'm not the same guy I was. I'm not looking for a fight with anyone. I can manage your office and give you good advice. And I do still have a few friends who could be real assets."

T.D. fidgeted. "When Larry called, I think he imagined this job would mostly be about helping out at the capitol. I'm not important enough to need a full-time assistant just to deal with state matters. The bulk of the job has to do with my other businesses. I sell insurance and run some used car lots—not very glamorous. The job involves helping me manage those businesses, plus being active in political matters, mostly during the legislative session. Not sure if that's the sort of thing you had in mind."

"No. Guess I hadn't thought about what the job would really be. Larry only talked about the political stuff. I know lots about politics. Not sure I'd be much use as a business person."

"You might surprise yourself. Managing a business has a lot in common with politics. I think you might be a natural—if you're still interested."

"T.D., I need a job. If you think I can be of help and do what you need done, I'm more than willing to give it a try."

"Have you stayed up with the latest goings-on around the capitol?"

"There is no joy in prison—hardest time of my life. If there was one thing that helped, it was the library. We were allowed access most days. I read the papers, the *Sun* and the *Journal*, every day. It was my lifeline back to reality." Ray paused. "Then my son, Tommy, got a job on the *Journal*, so of course I wanted to read his stuff. With one thing and another, I've spent a lot of time following everything that's been happening since I've been gone. Must say it looks like it's gotten even meaner than when I was around. Hard to believe."

T.D. smiled. "When can you start?"

After Ray's release from prison, he was surprised that Tracy Clark wanted anything to do with him. He'd confessed to her about his less-than-stellar track record with women. He suspected Tommy was one reason she stuck around. She and Tommy had become close when they tried together to save Judy Jackson from her growing mental problems. Both suffered when she was killed in a strange, horrible confrontation with the police.

In time, Ray began to realize he, Tracy and Tommy, without any discussion, were becoming a family.

Still, when she offered her spare bedroom, he balked at first. "Tracy, this is Bible-belt Oklahoma. You can't have a man living in your house. You'll be fired—maybe burned at the stake." He was pleased, but he wasn't going to let her take such a risk with her career, not to mention her reputation.

"Screw 'em! I don't care what anybody thinks or does. You need a place to stay, and I have an extra room—you should move in. Jesus, it is 1969! Half the damn population believes in free love. I will not be told what to do by a bunch of tight-assed fuddy-duddies." Her tone and the expression on her face suggested it wasn't in Ray's interest to argue.

"Okay, then. We'll think about it." Ray was smiling. "No matter what happens, it's very nice for you to offer. I owe you more than I can ever repay for the help you've given Tommy. I'm not sure what would have happened if you hadn't been there for him. You really are the greatest." He took her hand, held it for a while, then kissed it. They embraced. That evening Ray stayed over, but the spare room went unused.

Ultimately, they reached a compromise on the living situation. They would pretend Ray moved in strictly out of necessity while he looked for his own place. No matter what rumors might fly, if they stuck to their story, it was likely the weak-kneed manager at Tracy's TV station wouldn't have the nerve to fire her. And because moral standards for women were different from those for men, only her reputation was at risk. Ray's, if anything, would likely be enhanced. Within days, it felt completely natural. They had Tommy over for dinner, and it really did feel like they were a family.

5

BOMBS AND BASEBALL

"Hey, Vince, what brings you to my home away from home?" Tommy's preferred work location was the press room in the capitol building, mostly because few reporters used it.

"Your good buddy Mitch Douglas called the paper and asked to see me. June said I should stop by and let you know what's going on. She did make it clear you were not to go there with me."

"Have any idea what he wants?"

"Nope. But my guess is it's not good for the paper. He's still being investigated for fraud or bribes, or something along those lines, regarding the missing funds from the highway department. And according to my sources, he thinks it's entirely because of you and the *Journal.*"

Tommy debated joining Vince, no matter what the assistant city editor thought. But it would just create more trouble. Douglas, during a fit of rage months before over a bill that threatened to collapse his brother's carefully legislated financial advantages in the highway paving business, had pitched Tommy against the wall of his office and threatened two Capitol Police officers with a sidearm. And he'd gotten away with it. "Well, let me know what happens. Anything else going on?"

"Yeah, got a lead on an airman found dead on the base. The

paper got an anonymous tip claiming the guy was murdered and that the brass at Tinker is covering it up. I called out there a couple of days ago and asked to speak to Langston." General Brad Langston was in charge of the sprawling air base in eastern Oklahoma County. "They were all friendly until I mentioned what I wanted to talk about, and suddenly everything went cold. Said I'd have to see the information officer, a Lieutenant Davis, and hung up. Within the hour, Mister Anderson was down at my desk asking me why I was bothering the Tinker brass. Kind of weird. That was the first time I really talked to the paper's owner, and he's asking me why I'm doing my job. What do you think that's about?"

"Don't know. Anderson's friends with most of the higher-ups at Tinker. But I'm not sure that'd be reason enough for him to want to shut you down. What happened?"

"He told me to lay off of the story. So I did. Then yesterday Fred comes to see me and says I should go out to Tinker and meet with the information officer." Fred Simpson was the city editor and the primary force behind the day-to-day operation of the *Journal*. "So, I've got another appointment for this afternoon."

"Mind if I tag along?"

"Once I finish with Douglas, I'll swing back by and we can head out, okay?"

"Yep, see you in a bit." Tommy had been on the huge base a couple of times. Once was during an open house when he was a kid. It was vast to his young eyes, like another world full of mysteries and monster airplanes the size of buildings. He remembered getting autographs from Air Force officers like they were baseball players or movie stars.

Soon, Vince was back. "Douglas wasn't there. He left a message that he had to cancel and I should call him tomorrow. What a jerk," he spat.

"Maybe I should drop in on old Mitch and ask him why he's being so rude." Tommy smiled just thinking about it.

"One of these days you're going to get us both fired."

Tommy followed Vince to the *Journal* headquarters so he could drop off his car before the short drive to the base entrance. There they joined a long line of cars stopping as directed by signs bearing instructions enforced by serious Air Police who, depending on occupants or identities, would salute and allow access or review IDs.

An AP approached Vince's car. "Identification, please." He looked over their licenses, eyed the two men, and handed them back. "Why are you wanting to enter the base, sir?"

Vince explained he had an appointment with Lieutenant Davis, the information officer, and that he was a reporter for the *OK Journal,* and so was Tommy. The AP looked unhappy. He went to a clipboard and scanned it. He entered the small building next to the entrance, made a call, and returned.

"Go to the third building on your left, park in front. That is the Information Office. Do not go anywhere else. Do you understand, sir?"

"Yes."

Entering this well-guarded and secret place gave Tommy an uncomfortable sensation of surrendering control. These well-armed people now decided, efficiently and with no visible emotion, what he could and couldn't do. Make a false move, and something bad would happen. No "how you doin'?" It was all business. Sorry I shot you, but it was my duty. Tommy shivered.

Vince looked over. "You okay?"

"Yeah, I guess. This place gives me the heebie-jeebies."

They parked and entered a building topped by a sign that read, "Information Office." Upon entering, they were greeted by a very attractive young woman in civilian dress. "Welcome, Mister Young, Mister Jacks. We appreciate you coming out to see us. Would you like some coffee, water, or soda?"

Wow. They had gone from "next step: strip search" to a warm and friendly greeting from a beauty. They were shown to a leather couch to wait for the lieutenant, who didn't take long. He entered the room and warmly shook their hands. He was tall, with perfectly groomed hair and a broad, engaging smile. It seemed one of the requirements to work in the Information Office was to look good while you did it. The lieutenant led them into his office. "What can I do for you today, gentlemen?"

Vince put on his best reporter's face. "We received a tip that a body's been found on the base, and it might've been that of a murder victim. Can you give us any information?"

"Where'd the tip come from?" Some of the warmth had left the room.

"It was anonymous."

"So, based on some unsubstantiated anonymous tip, you've been hassling the commanding general's office?"

"I don't believe one phone call really constitutes hassling." Vince glanced at Tommy—this was not going well.

"At any given time, we may have as many as eight thousand soldiers and airmen on this base, and on occasion, someone will die. We have Air Police who handle any circumstances where there need to be investigations. This is a federal facility, and the local police have no jurisdiction. And the local press has a very, very limited right to question any of our procedures. There are often national security issues at stake. So, gentlemen, I appreciate you coming out and talking to us, but we have no information that we can provide to you at this time."

If there had been some kind of chute to deliver them to the front of the base like dirty laundry, it would have been triggered at that moment. Instead, they were politely shown the door, and within seconds found themselves standing outside.

"Well, I don't care what the sign says, that is not an 'Information Office.'" Tommy gave Vince a grin. "Let's get the hell out of here."

They headed back to the *Journal* building. "Does it ever feel like everybody hates you?" Vince had a serious look.

Tommy laughed. "No! I've never had that feeling in my life. Must just be you, Vince."

Monopoly night! Tommy couldn't believe it. His dad and Tracy had become doting parents in a matter of weeks. They wanted him to come over for dinner and play board games. He was actually starting to question their sanity. Maybe senility could set in fast. But Tracy seemed too young.

His dad answered the door and gave Tommy a hug; a thing that was going to take some getting used to. His dad remarried two times after his mother died, but the newer wives hadn't been motherly types. A benefit of that less-than-hands-on upbringing was that it made Tommy independent and resourceful. The downside was that he had a difficult time with emotions and relationships. "Dad—*Monopoly* night?"

"Tracy loves Monopoly. She's beaten my butt so many times,

she's looking for better competition. So just be nice and let her win." He smiled in a way so joyous it almost made Tommy cry.

"Not a chance. I'm going to fight tooth and nail for every dollar until I own everything!" Tommy jumped around in an ugly victory dance.

They had sausage lasagna and garlic bread, and it was delicious. Who knew that beautiful Tracy was a great cook besides everything else?

"How about a baseball game tomorrow night?"

"Dad, I don't need to be entertained. I had a great time tonight, and I want to do this more often. Even if Tracy beat me at Monopoly—do you think she cheats?" Tracy gave Tommy a jab on the shoulder, but squeezed his hand, too.

"Listen, Mister Wise-ass, my new employer thinks I'm doing a wonderful job, and his office has season tickets to the 89ers. He offered me three seats for tomorrow's game. Do you want to go see a baseball game or not?"

"Absolutely. I'll meet you at the ballpark."

A family.

Tommy did some research on the 89ers. He'd never been much into sports, partly from a lack of interest on his dad's part, but he was beyond holding a grudge. He'd also grown in odd spurts, so he'd never really felt coordinated, always sure he'd be horrible at any athletic activity. For those and other reasons, he'd never learned much about sports, including the big three: football, basketball, and baseball.

Being a reporter meant that if you didn't know something, you researched it. He headed to the library. Libraries had always been safe places for him. He'd spent hours studying and thinking in their protective comfort. His favorite was the one downtown, with its great tables and high ceilings. It felt like a church. For convenience, though, he'd also spent a lot of time in the neighborhood library off the Northwest Highway.

There he found magazine articles about the Oklahoma City 89ers baseball team, a Triple-A affiliate of the major league Houston Astros. The team played at All Sports Stadium, which seated about fifteen thousand people, on the State Fairgrounds. Tommy had seen it but had never been there. Selecting the local paper—the *OK Journal*, of course—he read about that night's game. They would play another Triple-A team out of Denver, and the 89ers were expected to win. He learned the home team's starting pitcher, Al Rosen, was having a career year and probably would be called up to the majors soon. The manager, Bill Nicholson, was an older baseball man, likely on his last team. He was quoted as saying he expected the team's star—third baseman, Ray Boone—to have a great game. Boone had been playing really well the last few months, but he was thirty-five and about done. His major league career had ended on a sub-par season with the Cleveland Indians, and he was expected to retire after his minor-league contract ran out at the end of the year. He was still hitting with a fair bit of power, but his legs were almost gone.

The 89ers had the best starting outfield in the minors, according to several sports magazines. Orlando Alvarez, Mario Diaz, and Domingo Cedeno were known in the baseball press as the "three amigos." All were expected to be called up by the parent club or traded soon. Minor league baseball teams were constantly changing, so there was little if any security for the players.

Then he found a *Sporting News* featuring a back-pages interview with Alvarez. It seemed clear he was ready to leave Oklahoma City. "I'm a good baseball player," the article quoted him as saying. "But the people here are all bigots, and I mean the people who own this team, and the management. I've asked to be traded, and if that doesn't happen, I'll have to just leave. Otherwise, something ugly is going to happen,".

Baseball might be America's national pastime, but it looked like trouble was brewing in America's heartland.

OK Journal

My View—Tommy Jacks

It's clear now: this is all my fault. Since my first day, or even further back than that, I've labored under a grand misapprehension that murder is a serious crime. That's my fault, I'll admit. People just get killed all the time, and probably a hundred times a day on TV. It's a natural thing, so what's the big deal?

Just ask Air Force Lt. Jeff Davis, the affable and photogenic Information Officer at Tinker Air Force Base. I'll quote what he said after reporters summoned the gumption to show up and ask him about a tip they'd received concerning a death on the base that might be a murder: "At any given time, we may have as many as 8,000 soldiers and airmen on this base, and on occasion, someone will die."

Well, shoot. Who'd have thought? And besides, Davis continued, whatever happens on the base, even if it might be murder, is the base's business, and not that of local police, local press, or anyone or anything else local. It's kind of like the Air Force's own little country there, south of town. Which is odd when you remember that they're here to protect our country. Or so we're told every time it seems convenient for someone to say so. 🦋

6

CRIME AND ERRORS

After a quick lunch of tasteless tacos, Tommy headed back to the capitol press room, thinking about baseball and the game tonight, and finding a little time for a nap. He found a cop sitting at one of the desks. No one else was there.

The officer stood. "Jacks?" He posed his question in a commanding voice. "My name is Captain Jefferson. If you have a minute, I'd like to talk to you."

Tommy's experiences with police since becoming a reporter had mostly been bad, so his heartbeat picked up its pace. "Sure. What can I do for you?"

Once the man spoke, though, Tommy relaxed a little. It didn't sound like the guy was there to arrest him or bludgeon him with a blunt instrument. "I've read your articles in the paper. Especially the ones about the chief." The captain hesitated, and he seemed nervous. "First, I want to make sure this is off the record. I'm sticking my neck out being here, but for right now I need you to agree that none of this gets into the paper, okay?"

"Okay—unless you tell me something I'm legally obligated to pass along. Reporters can keep secrets, and can definitely keep things out of the papers, but we aren't like priests or lawyers. What you tell me might not be covered by any legal privilege." Even to Tommy, he sounded like one of his journalism professors.

"Yeah, I know. I just don't want anything in the papers right now. I need your help."

Tommy sat down to listen.

Jefferson told him he joined the police force right after he got out of the Marines. He said he always wanted to be a cop and saw it as an honorable profession, a calling to protect citizens. Chief Underwood had been his commanding officer when he was first promoted to lieutenant. He'd been aggressive, and taught Jefferson a lot. "In a lot of ways, he was my hero. I trusted him completely." But things changed. Underwood was named chief, and suddenly became more concerned with politics than fighting crime. He also started living pretty high on the hog for a cop—even for a chief. He spent most of his time at charity events or political gatherings. A lot of the guys really got down on him, but Jefferson defended the chief, saying he was just making sure the police department would get the money it needed. Besides, he was the chief now, not just some cop on the beat.

Then things *really* changed, he said. Most organized crime in the area was controlled by a handful of groups, one led by Big Frank Martin. Jefferson said his goal was to put Martin behind bars. It was hard to make anything stick, though, because it wasn't like he was out in the street committing crimes himself. And he had an army of lawyers ready anytime the cops even looked at him sideways. But he'd thought he was getting closer—he knew some lowlifes who he thought might turn on Martin if he kept pushing them. If he could get one to testify against Martin, he could finally put him away. One day, about four years ago, Jefferson felt he was making progress when the chief called him into his office.

"This is where the shit hit the fan. He told me to back off of Martin—said we needed to concentrate on crimes that were really harming people. You're not going to believe this, but he said I should concentrate on drunk driving. I thought he was kidding. Once I realized he was serious, I sort of lost it. I told him I was not a goddamn traffic cop. Well, he got angry and ended the meeting, and the next morning I was transferred to traffic. I kept my rank, but now I really *was* a goddamn traffic cop."

Tommy was not sure what to make of Jefferson. "You've been in traffic the last four years?"

"Yeah. It's not all that bad actually, and at least it puts me in contact with real people, which I like. But this whole time I've kept my eye on my good pal, the chief, and I've accumulated quite a few documents that show that he's stepped in pretty regularly to help Martin or one of his thugs to avoid police attention. I've read your columns where you've raised the question of whether or not the chief is dirty. I believe I have proof that he is."

"You said this is off the record. Why are you telling me this?"

"I've decided I can't do anything to stop what's going on. Martin's left town, but I think the chief's maybe working with some of the people who are taking over some of his previous enterprises. I can't stop him because he *is* the police department. I thought about going to the mayor, but I think he could be on the take, too. Of course, there's the feds, but I honestly believe the FBI would arrest me if I took this story to them—I don't trust them at all. I can't go to the *Oklahoma Sun* because he and Gilmore are best buddies. So, what I'm suggesting is that I help you reveal the chief for what he really is. You write the stories, and I give you the supporting information to back them up. What do you say?"

Tommy hesitated. How could he know if Jefferson was telling the truth? What if this was a set-up? Albright had been set up by Gilmores' men years before, and it cost him his job. His dad had been set up by a team of liars, and he'd gone to prison. He didn't want to lose Jefferson and his evidence, but he couldn't publish anything until he had proof. There was also something about Jefferson that seemed too pat, like his story had been scripted. He needed to talk to Albright, get him involved. This was out of his league. "Captain, I definitely want to work with you to get this information about the chief out to the public. But before I write anything, I need to see the documents you're talking about. I don't know you. I have to be careful."

"Of course. I understand. Let's meet again in a couple of days and I'll bring you some documents."

Jefferson didn't want to come back to the capitol. They agreed to meet in the south parking lot of Sears, on Pennsylvania Avenue and 23rd Street, in two days, at five o'clock.

It was a little early, but Tommy decided to head out to the ballpark. He was surprised to feel as excited as he did, like a kid—it felt good. He'd finished his column and called it in, so work was over for the day. He'd always wanted to be a journalist, and at first developed an unrealistic idea about what that might mean. He'd learned on the job that the primary goal seemed to be to get something written to meet your deadline—more of a job than an adventure.

Approaching the ballpark, he could see police cars had blocked the entrance to the parking lot. He pulled up and rolled down his window. "What's going on?"

"Game's canceled. Once they decide on a make-up date, it'll be announced."

Tommy looked around. Canceling a ballgame was one thing. Having cops block off the entrance was something else entirely. "Why's it been canceled?"

"Look buddy, there's no baseball tonight, so just turn around and be on your way." Every cop he met seemed to have a short fuse, and it was getting tiresome.

"I'm meeting people here. Can I wait over there?" Tommy indicated part of the lot close by.

"Yeah, I guess that's okay. Just stay in your car until they show. Then you have to leave."

He pulled in and spotted more police cars, an ambulance, and barricades around the stadium.His reporter's instinct told him to get out and walk down there to see if someone would talk to him.

He decided to wait until his dad and Tracy showed up. Tommy got out of his car to make sure his dad saw him, and to hear better. A whole line of cars pulled up to be told the game was off, and not everyone was pleased. One guy, who appeared to have had a few pre-game beers, was arrested for shouting about how the government shouldn't be allowed to shut down baseball in a free country.

Tommy picked out Tracy's car down the line. Traffic moved at a snail's pace, so he walked to meet them.

She rolled her window down. "What kind of trouble are

you in now, sweetie?" She was being playful, but Tommy understood the implication.

"The game's canceled. Must be because of some kind of crime, what with all the cops. They'll tell you once you get up there that you have to leave and they don't know anything."

His dad leaned over to say, "Hop in, we can go get something to eat."

"I'm going to try to find out what's going on. I think I can drive around behind the stadium and get closer. Might not learn anything, but it's worth a try. I'll call you later." Tommy started to leave.

"You be careful. Don't get into any trouble." Tracy's voice was full of concern.

The cops seemed to have a myopic sense of access, blocking the main entrance and ignoring other places. Tommy couldn't get into the parking lot because of the closed gates, but he could walk across the lot without anyone noticing.

Near the first base entrance he could see activity—and a body on the ground. It was covered by a sheet that appeared to have blood on it. Forensics people searched nearby, apparently collecting evidence. No question in Tommy's mind—it was a crime scene, and almost certainly a murder.

The police spotted him, and one approached.

"Sorry, sir, you can't be in this area. I'll need you to leave now." While direct and firm, he didn't seem to be angry, which was a relief.

"Yeah, sure. What's happening? Somebody get hurt?"

"Yep, got hurt real bad. This is police business now, so you need to leave." Tommy waved his understanding and started walking in the other direction, only far enough to be ignored again, so he could turn toward the back of the stadium where two men stood by a gate, smoking.

They wore uniforms indicating they worked for the 89ers. "Hiya. What's all the excitement out front?"

Both shrugged. "They don't tell us much. Just that the game is canceled and we have to clean up the kitchens before we leave."

"Well, I was just out front, and I saw a body on the ground. Cops everywhere." Tommy almost asked for a cigarette to make himself seem more like part of their little group. But he didn't smoke, and he probably would have choked to death in front of them. He just smiled.

"That's what we heard. One other guy said it was Ray Boone. Said someone shot him. Man, that's going to cause a *lot* of problems. We could be shut down for weeks. That means no money for us."

Tommy knew the concern of living from one paycheck to the next. "Probably not that long. I bet it's just a couple of days at most. Baseball will go on."

Murder at the ballpark—there was something not only unsettling about that, but very un-American. Tommy needed to find a pay phone to let someone know about his scoop.

7

LAWYERS AND MORE LAWYERS

Denny's was jam-packed, with people lined up for tables. Over in a corner, at the largest booth in the place, sat Taylor Albright and his papers, unconcerned that he took up a table for six all by himself. Tommy joined him, uninvited.

"Morning, Taylor. Where are your bodyguards?"

"Good morning, Tommy. I see you've recovered from your bad day; back to your usual annoying ways."

Tommy put on a shocked look. "Annoy you, by asking a simple question? How can that be?"

"Like right now, you're annoying me. I'm sitting here minding my own business, and you come along and upset me. Why?" To someone listening, it would be hard to see the level of friendship that existed between the young reporter and the older tabloid gossip. But it was there—if you squinted.

"Okay, let's just start over. Hello, Taylor."

"Hello, Tommy. What's up?"

"I need your advice, and maybe your help." Tommy always treated Albright with great caution, like defusing a bomb that might go off at any moment.

Taylor put his paper down, sat up straighter, and put on a professorial face. "Please, young man, tell me all about your troubles."

"Look, I'm not joking. A Captain Jefferson from the Oklahoma City Police Department came to see me at the capitol press room and offered documentation proving Chief Underwood has been helping Big Frank Martin and his goons escape police investigations for years. He wants me to put this stuff into my column and expose the chief."

"That's too good to be true. Somebody's setting you up. Do you know anything about this Jefferson?"

"At this point, only what he's told me." Tommy told Albright everything Jefferson said about himself, and about his upcoming meeting with him.

"Yep, none of that smells right. Go to the meeting and get the documents, but don't commit to anything and don't say anything you wouldn't want repeated. I'll investigate this guy and see what I can find out. By the way, Mister Wise-ass, you asked about Max and Nathan. For your information, they're in town. Could be they're watching you right now, wondering if they should attack. So, if I were you, I'd be damned careful."

Tommy couldn't help himself—he looked around. When he looked back, Albright was smiling. Max Jones and Nathan Oliver were the best-dressed and most courteous thugs the world had ever seen. Taylor met them while they were hiding from something or someone that was never identified, as guests of Big Frank Martin. As a result of a connection with Tommy's dad, they became Albright's bodyguards after he was physically threatened during the gubernatorial campaign of 1962. Being from New York City like Albright, the three became friends despite other differences. During a very tense period while Martin was still around, they'd gone back to the comforts of the Big Apple but told Albright they would return if needed. And now they had.

"Have you talked to my dad lately?"

"Nope. I guess he's still healing, and I'm probably just a reminder of bad times. Anyway, I should call him. Is he still staying with you?"

"He moved into Tracy Clark's house," Tommy said neutrally.

Albright raised his eyebrows. "Well, that's interesting. What's going on there, or is that a bad question to ask the kid?"

Tommy chuckled. "Nah, I think it's great. They're very important to me, so having them in one place is convenient, if nothing else. My dad seems happy." That last statement was said with a wry look.

There was a pause. "Well, that's great. I'm happy for them, and you. It's good to hear about something that's working out."

"He's working for T.D. McFadden now, one of the Oklahoma County reps. He helps with the political stuff and other businesses McFadden owns, like car lots. It was kind of strange, but the other night I had dinner with Tracy and Dad, and he was talking about his new job and mentioned that they did a lot of business with Dealin' Dave." He saw Albright look up and frown. "I didn't say anything about your issues with him. I just thought you ought to know about that. You might want to call and talk to Dad about what's going on."

"Yeah, maybe I should." Albright said, distracted.

Just as Tommy was thinking about heading out, Joe Louongo dropped into the booth. Without so much as a word of greeting, he started in.

"This fuckin' town has the worst police force on the whole fuckin' planet. I've just come from downtown, and those bastards had the balls to threaten me with jail—can you believe that shit? I'm down there doin' my duty for my client, who they have held way beyond what is allowed, and they come after me. Told me if I didn't shut the fuck up, they were gonna throw my ass in jail—that is illegal, immoral, and unconsti- fuckin'-tutional. I'm filing suit this afternoon. I'll have that asshole sergeant and the goddamn chief in court before they know what hit 'em. Bastards can't threaten me!"

By the time he'd finished his outburst, most of Denny's was listening. Somehow the offensive language was such a natural fit with Louongo's New Jersey wise-guy image, it *almost* wasn't offensive. But he became aware people were listening, made a "tip-of-the-hat" gesture, and signaled for a waitress. His audience returned to their breakfasts.

"Well, good morning to you, Mister Louongo." Albright smiled. He enjoyed a good show.

Tommy jumped in, always the reporter. "Who's your client?"

"Sorry, nosy Mr. Reporter, no scoops for you this morning." Louongo and Tommy had a strained relationship, like most involving the lawyer.

"Off the record." Tommy was now just curious.

"Well, you're goin' to know about it soon enough anyway. My innocent client is Billy Ray Watts, owner of the 89ers baseball team. They've charged him with the murder of Ray Boone."

Tommy left for the capitol press room. It was obvious Albright and Louongo had planned to meet at Denny's, and just as obvious that as long as Tommy stayed, they weren't going to discuss the reason for their meeting. Besides, if Watts had been charged, it was public record, and all bets were off. He called June and reported what he knew.

Within minutes, she called back to confirm to him that the 89ers' owner was charged with the murder of his star third baseman. She told him police gave no other information, like motive or a murder weapon, and Vince was headed to police headquarters to see if he could learn more.

Since politics, not murder, was Tommy's beat, he decided to take a tour of the capitol and see what he could learn. The session was heating up, with several controversies brewing. Money—or more accurately, lack of it—drove most conflicts. Politicians of all stripes loved to spend other people's money; it was one of their natural talents. But almost all ran on campaigns to cut taxes and increase spending because it kept them in office. Of course, they never had enough money, and as a result, provided a low-cost, inefficient, and ineffective government. Poor roads, poor schools, poor criminal-justice system, and lower taxes on the rich were not a wise plan, but you would still be re-elected because voters didn't seem to understand that the elites, and the news organizations that supported them, really didn't give a damn.

"Hey, Tommy. Long time, no see." A very large security guard extended his huge hand in greeting.

"Bart, how you doin'?"

"Not bad. Glad to see ya. I was so sorry about Judy. It still makes me so sad, I almost cry. Hope you're okay."

"Yeah, thanks. It's getting better, just takes some time for all of us." Tommy wanted this phase of grieving to be over. But he knew many people were upset over her death, and would be for a while yet. "Any juicy stories you can share about our leaders?"

Bart grinned. "No way, Tommy. I'm part of the establishment. We're not even supposed to talk to the press. Hey, have
you met the new guy from the *Sun?* Name's Mike Sanders.
Kind of a young guy like you. Pretty standoffish. Guess he
knows what he's doin', but he's not very friendly. He asked me
about you the other day, said he wanted to meet you. Maybe
you're a star now."

"I haven't. Understand he moved here from the *Denver Post.*
Kind of sounded like a demotion to me, but who knows? And
I'm no star. But establishment or not, keep your eye out for those
juicy stories, I need all the help I can get." Tommy gave Bart a
gentle slap on his massive back and headed down the hall.

While touring offices of representatives and senators, he
spotted Mitch Douglas at the end of a hallway. The representative from Perkins gave Tommy the finger and ducked into his
office. *Mature.* Tommy turned and headed the other way. This
unreasonable conflict with Douglas needed to be resolved, but
damned if he knew how.

He dropped in at Senator Evans's office and chatted with
Gail Collins. She'd been another good friend of Judy's. They
talked mostly about nothing until it started to remind Tommy
of the past. He did learn about some hearings the next week he
thought he should attend. He headed back to the press room
to call June and see if she knew anything about where things
stood with Douglas.

"We just received a copy of a lawsuit filed this morning. It
names the paper and Bill personally. And you, too, Tommy.
Sorry."

"What does that mean? Will the paper defend me?"

"Not one hundred percent sure. I'd think you'd want to hire

your own lawyer, and then maybe they could work with the paper's attorneys. But, trust me, I'm not the one to give you legal advice."

What kind of bullshit was that? Hire his own attorney? *Like I've got money lying around.* The only lawyer he knew was the very possibly crazy Joe Louongo. The paper should pay for whatever defense he needed. "Okay. If you hear anything else, let me know. Douglas is acting weird out here."

They talked about his deadlines and stories he was working on, but he only half paid attention. He was still thinking about the lawsuit and what it might mean for him. He was poorly paid, and he owned almost nothing other than his junker car, so maybe he didn't need to worry. Then he realized what it could mean to his still-new career if he lost a defamation lawsuit. He needed impartial advice.

He called his dad. After going over the details, Ray offered a solution.

"Hire Larry Alexander. I know him, and he'll know about you. He's the best, and completely independent of Bill and the paper. He'll represent your interests and no one else's, and you can trust him completely, on my word. As far as money, if you need some right now, I can help—and don't say no. You have to protect yourself. But beyond that, I know Bill Anderson better than you do. He'll help you. You may still need your own lawyer, even if the paper says they'll defend you along with them, but I can almost guarantee you Bill will reimburse you. If for some strange reason he doesn't, we'll figure out a way to cover it. Make an appointment with Larry right now and let me know what he says."

Tommy called the lawyer's office and spoke to someone

with the most sensuous voice he'd ever heard. She said her name was Patricia White and she was Mister Alexander's assistant. She put Tommy on hold while she consulted Alexander, then came back on the phone.

"Mister Jacks, Mister Alexander said he has an opening tomorrow at one."

Tommy almost didn't answer—he was so enchanted by her voice he was not listening to her words. "Sure, okay. Tomorrow at one. Okay." He sounded like an idiot.

OK Journal

My View—Tommy Jacks

Meanwhile, back at the highway department ranch, Gov. Rick Butler is pulling the strings to get Marvin Truman appointed as the new director after the debacle that saw the firing of the last one, Hobart Mitchell, along with two employees of the department, to boot. You might recall that state Rep. Mitch Douglas, R-Perkins, figured into the mess in a way I'm not allowed to talk about for the present because he's started a legal action in the matter.

Back to Truman: Butler's got powerful help in the person of state Sen. Gene Rapier, probably the most powerful Democrat in the state, out of McAlester. He's sponsoring a bill to change the requirements for the position, removing a stipulation that the highway director must be a civil engineer.

Why's he doing that? "I'm just doing this for (Sen. Ben) Nichols," Rapier said with a shrug. "I believe it has something to do with a constituent of his." Yeah. Everybody's just helping each other out.

Turns out Truman, who does live in Nichols' district, was also a major contributor to his campaigns for state representative some years back, and the Senate more recently. Aren't we just a nice bunch of people here in Oklahoma? 🥀

8
LEGAL ANGELS AND ASSHOLES

Tommy stopped at the 7-Eleven just down from his apartment to pick up a copy of the *Journal*. He wasn't going to see Albright, so he got a not-so-fresh donut and coffee. The attendant recognized him.

"How 'bout the owner of the 89ers killing his best third baseman? Can you believe that? Shit, if he didn't like him, he should have just cut him. Killing ballplayers just ain't right." The serious look on his face suggested he wasn't kidding, and Tommy decided he would have to start going elsewhere for life's little necessities.

His recently acquired knowledge about baseball gave him the confidence to try a joke. "Yeah. Can't just shoot people for having bad knees." The clerk just stared.

Tommy sat in his car to read Vince's story about the ballpark murder. There were a few new items in it, and Vince did a good job at laying out what was known, or what the cops would admit. It seems Billy Ray Watts was seen having a very animated, perhaps angry, conversation with Ray Boone a short time before Boone's body was found. Billy Ray was in his office when the police went to question him and, by one account, pulled a gun on them before he could be subdued. Another account—this one from Joe Louongo, Billy Ray's attorney—

contended that the cops stormed his office with drawn pistols, never bothering to identify themselves as police, and Billy Ray's natural reaction was to defend himself against armed intruders with one of his many collectable Confederate Army sidearms.

Vince also quoted a worker who witnessed the arrest, who said Watts yelled at the arresting officers, "I'm a personal friend of President Nixon, and you're going to pay dearly for this outrage!" Next to the article was a photo of Billy Ray's office, with an autographed picture of the president.

Tommy spent most of the morning in the capitol press room working on his column and talking with the few people who dropped by. Some asked if he'd met Mike Sanders yet; he hadn't. Sanders was the replacement for Tony Walters, the political reporter for the *Oklahoma Sun* whom Judy killed—more history not far enough in the past for his comfort. He decided it was time to head downtown to see Larry Alexander.

The office was on the fifth floor of a glamorous old building on the corner of Park Avenue and Main. Every aspect reflected a stylish class seldom present in modern buildings. The elevator alone had more fine wood and brass than a rich man's coffin. He felt underdressed.

"Good afternoon, are you Mister Jacks?" The voice posing the question was the same mesmerizing one he'd heard on the phone, and it came from one of the loveliest women he'd ever seen—angelic, with a gorgeous smile, blonde hair, and large, sparkling blue eyes.

"Eh, yes, I'm me. I mean, yes, I'm Mister Jacks. Actually, Tommy."

"Well, 'Actually Tommy,' have a seat and I'll let Mister Alexander know you're here." She smiled. He thought he might faint. He considered leaving before she could come back. Was it even possible to behave more like a fool? My god, you'd think he was back in junior high, stammering just because a pretty girl smiled at him. *Well, pretty* and *clever,* he amended. He sat down on the couch and held his head. She returned to show him to Alexander's elegant office.

"Tommy Jacks, it's great to meet you. I've known your dad a long time, and he's talked about you often. Have a seat. Want anything to drink?"

"No, I'm fine. Thank you."

"So, tell me what's going on with this lawsuit." Larry was one of the world's great listeners and knew how to make people feel comfortable.

In minutes, Tommy told him everything he knew. "I wasn't sure if I even needed a lawyer, but my dad insisted that I should at least ask for advice."

"You do need a lawyer. First thing we need is for you to sign a representation agreement. I'm going to set my fee at one dollar. It's just a token payment for now, but it makes me officially your lawyer, which makes this a confidential, privileged conversation. I'm sure you're worried about money, but don't be. I don't work for nothing, but until we know for sure what's going on, it won't be a factor—except for the dollar." Larry smiled.

Tommy immediately felt safer. "What happens next?"

"Mostly nothing. I'll need to get a copy of the statement of claim and talk to the *Journal's* attorney. At first blush, unless something surprising turns up, I think we can be in the background while the *Journal* pushes the court case along. That means almost no cost to you. Now, Douglas's attorney can throw a monkey wrench into that by naming you in a separate lawsuit if he wants to, but that would cost them more money for no real gain. I think in a week or so we should schedule a session with a court stenographer and have you tell your story before anyone asks for a deposition. That way we get all the facts out on the table so we can look them over and see if there's anything we need to be concerned about. I'll have Patsy put something together in the next week or two." Larry smiled. "Remember, if anything happens, you let me know immediately. Also, I'd avoid contact with Douglas. I know your work involves covering the legislature, but just stay away from any direct contact with him."

Before leaving, he managed a conversation with Patsy that involved complete sentences—although she still caught him just staring. They exchanged contact information, and she typed a standard rep agreement for him to sign.

"So, Tommy, all that's left is for you to pay the dollar."

"This is a little embarrassing, but I don't have any money on me right now. I can go get a dollar and come right back." He was stranded in idiot city, in front of her.

"It's okay." Perfect smile. "Here—I'll loan you a dollar." She reached into her desk, took a dollar out of her purse, and paper-clipped it to the agreement. "Now you owe *me.*"

Tommy couldn't remember if he said anything after that or not. He more or less floated all the way to his car.

Back at the press room, Tommy was surprised to see someone at one of the desks. More often than not, he was the only one there.

"Hey, you must be Jacks. I'm Mike Sanders, new guy at the *Sun*. Heard a lot about you." Mike Sanders was short and overweight. He seemed to snarl, although Tommy reasoned it could have been some odd kind of muscle twitch. Still, he didn't seem friendly. He did get up, but didn't offer a handshake.

"Yep, that's me. Welcome aboard. Need anything, just let me know." Tommy started toward the back to an open desk.

"Probably won't be needing anything from you. Understand you're new at this stuff, and your daddy got you some cushy assignment writing a gossip column. So, if you need my help, forget it—I don't know anything about gossip columns." His pudgy face turned a shade of pink, as if the effort of speaking took extra oxygen. "I just interviewed Mitch Douglas. He says you'll be sweeping floors pretty soon because he's suing you and your two-bit paper for libel. Any comment?"

Tommy was tall and slender, with wide shoulders and noticeable muscles. The contrast with Sanders was laughable. He looked the worm in the face. "Yeah. Fuck you."

"Not sure my paper will let me run that quote, but I'll try. Douglas also said you attacked him—that true, Mister Daddy's Boy?"

Tommy, in a move that surprised even himself, grabbed Sanders under his arms, lifted him off the floor, shoved him against the wall, and got in his face. "Don't know what your problem is, asshole, but I won't put up with your bullshit. So, you stay away from me, got it?" The little man looked surprised at Tommy's strength. He nodded. Tommy let him slide to the floor, walked back to the desk, and sat down.

Sanders remained on the floor a few minutes, getting his

wits about him. "You've really screwed up now. I'm calling the police. You can't just go around attacking people anytime you want. What's wrong with you?"

Tommy looked up. "Lots, you little slime. Get the fuck out of here while you still can."

Sanders scrambled to his feet and left.

He returned with a Capitol Police officer in tow, noticeably winded. "There he is! Arrest him, now!"

The officer looked at Sanders like he was a complete idiot. "I'll talk to him. Why don't you go somewhere else, okay? If I need anything more from you, I'll give you a call."

"What, are you covering this up? What kind of fake cop are you? This whole state is full of morons. Steve Marsh warned me about Jacks. Within minutes of meeting him, he attacks me, and you treat him like he's the victim. Are you stupid or what?"

The officer just looked at Sanders. "I know Jacks. So, I'm going to issue you a warning. You cause any more trouble around here, you'll be banned from the capitol for being disruptive to the legislative process. Now I think it'd be best if you went someplace else." The tension in the officer's voice suggested Sanders was close to being attacked twice within the hour. The reporter mumbled something about morons and left.

"Did you attack that little creep, Jacks?"

"Only a little. Not nearly enough."

"Well, other than a thumbs-up, we'll just forget about it." The officer shook his head and left.

Wondering why he hadn't thought of it sooner, Tommy headed to Risso's, a not-so-famous Italian restaurant run by a Mexican family named Lopez. It featured a more famous backroom bar Tommy's dad frequented back in the day. It was close to the capitol on Lincoln Boulevard, and a favorite watering hole while the legislature was in session.

Tommy wasn't a big drinker, but it was a comforting place where he felt welcome. "Tommy Jacks, where the hell have you been? I haven't seen you in months." That came from Larry Lopez, the owner, and an old friend of the Jacks family. "Come in, come in. Drinks or pizza?"

Tommy's grieving had kept him away from one of his favorite places for too long. Good food and strong drink—he should have dropped by before. "Well, Larry, I think first a couple of drinks, then a large sausage pizza to go. How've you been?"

"Business is tough. You can get booze almost anywhere, it seems like, and pizza's sold at the 7-Eleven or delivered. Without the legislature being in session, it's tough to cover my overhead. But things are better right now, so I'll worry about tomorrow, tomorrow."

"Let me buy you a drink, Larry."

"*Gracias.*" He signaled the bartender and ordered their drinks. They talked about business, Tommy's dad, politics, and the general futility of life. By the time he got his pizza and headed home, Tommy was feeling better. Risso's was better than therapy.

9
PROMOTION AND DEMOTION

When Ray Jacks was chairman of the state Democratic Party, he was always out of the office working candidates and donors. Now he was special assistant to T.D. McFadden and was expected to be in the office and available. It took some getting used to. The title of special assistant didn't mean anything in itself, but when T.D. introduced him to the office he made it clear Ray was the number two man in the business, which wasn't large. A staff of twelve handled the insurance part and administrative duties for his three used car lots, with another fifteen employees among them.

T.D.'s role as a state representative was one he took seriously. And of course, it was good for business. He had insurance contracts with a lot of politicians and the businesses they owned. That bent the rules a bit, and one of Ray's duties was to make sure the political beast could never bite T.D. in the ass without warning. T.D. was a good politician, which by definition meant he wasn't exactly pure. Ray, no innocent himself, thought T.D. was probably more ethical than most.

And being a lone wolf by nature, Ray found office gossip and infighting tiresome. For the first few weeks he just ignored them in favor of getting his head around exactly what was going on. He had run something akin to a business—the state party—but details were not his forte. He was much more comfortable in bars, talking politics or sports. He did have a knack for salesmanship—he could sell damn near anything to anybody because he could get them to believe in whatever he was selling.

After a period of observation, Ray decided to appoint a middle-aged, somewhat dumpy woman named Loretta Lynch as office manager. There were two very attractive women in the office who had expected to get the post, or so their less-than-subtle flirting with Ray indicated. Ray immediately gave Loretta complete power to fire, hire, demote or behead anyone she chose.

Loretta managed with a no-nonsense approach. Within days, fighting for status stopped. She fired one of the most attractive—and annoying—women on her second day in power. Soon everyone was all about business.

T.D. saw the changes and gave Ray the credit he deserved. Still, after a few weeks, Ray began to realize he'd made a mistake. The incredibly efficient Loretta was completely in charge, and there was little need for him. That created some risk, but also some reward—he was unshackled from the desk. He began to spend more time at the capitol, making the rounds—he knew just about everyone who was anyone. There were new faces because he'd been gone for some time, but he was quick to make friends, and even some of his enemies tended to like him. He couldn't have told you why political gossip was more palatable than office gossip, but he enjoyed it more. He was also getting a better picture of how Tommy fit into that convoluted world. Several people mentioned him and how much they enjoyed reading his columns. He felt the glow of fatherly pride, even if it was in some sense unearned.

"Hey, Tommy. How are ya?" He knew he was invading his son's sanctuary, but he wanted to see him.

"Dad? What are you doing here?"

"Don't worry. I won't make a habit of dropping in on you. Just down here working in T.D.'s office today and thought I'd let you know I'll probably be around a bit more. Fair warning, okay?"

"I didn't mean you couldn't drop in. Come in. Ever been up here before?"

"Couple times. Hearing good things from people about your work. Lots of compliments."

"Well, you ought to read the letters to the editor about my columns. I'm surprised that many god-fearing Okies use that kind of language. At least it keeps those letters out of the paper." They both chuckled.

"I'm proud of you, Tommy." His dad's voice broke a little. He gave his son a hug and left.

Later that day, Tommy headed to the *Journal's* headquarters in the suburbs to meet with June and Fred, which was out of the ordinary. Usually Fred let June handle such meetings alone.

"Tommy, come in. Have a seat." It was also unusual to have the meeting in the conference room, or for Fred to be concerned for Tommy's comfort.

He felt wary. June said hello and squeezed Tommy's hand in a comforting gesture. My god, were they going to fire him?

"We've got several topics we need to cover today. None of them bad, so relax. But we do have a lot of ground to cover, and

I thought it best if we did it all at once. First, I want to let you know everyone is really pleased with your work. You've taken on a lot, and you've done well. So, you're going to be put on the payroll. No more measuring to determine your pay. June can go over the numbers with you, but it will be a substantial raise and steady pay. Congratulations."

Nothing wrong with that. "Thanks. That'll make it a lot easier. Thanks, very much."

"You've earned it. Just keep up the good work. The next matter has to do with Senator Knight. He's in town dealing with his wife's death. Bill thought it would be good if we could get an interview with him. He and the senator go back a ways, and when Bill called him, he sounded agreeable to having someone do a short interview exclusively for the *Journal.* We think it could be good for you. I know you haven't done a feature like that with us, but Bill thinks your youth perspective is great, and he wants this to be a feather in your cap. So, June is in the process of getting something scheduled in the next few days."

"I don't know, Fred. I'm at my best out in the field chasing a story. I don't even know much about him other than his wife died. Maybe it'd be better if Vince did it." Tommy couldn't figure out why they would ask him to do the story. Hell, they'd just taken him off stringer status, and now he was supposed to sit down, one on one, with a United States senator?

"Look, Tommy. This is coming from Bill. He thinks you're a real talent. And this will be a front-page feature. He thinks it'll help build your profile and support your column. We'll help any way we can. And you can consult with Vince, or Albright, or even your dad. You won't have to wing it. You'll be prepared. You're a fresh face, and this could be a big break."

"You said it's gonna be in just a few days. I really need help, or this could be embarrassing."

"It'll work out. As soon as we're done here and you talk with June about payroll, I'll get you together with Vince and he can help you. You'll do just fine."

Easy for him to say, Tommy thought, but he nodded and smiled. He could always quit. Maybe he could be a bartender at Risso's.

"Next up is a correction on an oversight on my part. I should've told you immediately, once that lawsuit from Douglas showed up, that the paper—even Bill himself—will help with any costs you have. You won't get stuck with a legal bill. Everyone thinks Larry Alexander is a great choice, and Bill even said he's a good addition to the team for the paper. Nobody thinks anything'll come of this lawsuit—it's just harassment by Douglas because he's such an ass. But we don't want you to worry about money while this proceeds, okay?"

"Sure, that's great. Thank Mister Anderson for me. I really appreciate it. I'm not exactly rolling in dough." Chuckles all around.

"About to the end of our agenda. You went to Tinker with Vince the other day, and I guess you experienced the official cold shoulder about the body found on the base. June and I talked about this and decided the direct approach was not going to get us anywhere. We decided to ask Chuck Branson—he does the police beat—to do a little digging. Chuck was hired because of his experience working on the base newspaper. He was in the Air Force and was stationed at Tinker, and when his time was up, he stayed in town and took a job on their paper out there. Then, when we started up, he joined us. So, he's an insider and knows the ropes. And he's learned a lot. We now know the person killed was a Sergeant Kent Milton, and that he was stabbed—numerous times. Someone really wanted the guy dead. And the topper is, he wasn't killed where he was found. He'd been dead for days when his body was discovered."

"Wow. Why are they covering all that up?"

"Chuck thinks the brass believes the sergeant was smuggling drugs. Some of Chuck's drinking buddies said a lot of people knew Milton was the guy who managed the cargo on the transport planes. It seems they made regular trips to some destinations in South America, delivering secret cargo. The rumor from the bar guys was it involved the CIA."

"What are you going to do with that?"

"Not sure. Obviously, this is background information and completely, one hundred percent not confirmed— literally bar talk. All we have is a reasonable supposition the crime was murder and the Air Force brass are covering it up. And Chuck said most of the bar gossips thought the drugs were being sold in the city. Why they thought so, no one said. If Chuck's information is right, there's someone in our town buying a lot of illegal drugs. It could be a huge story. We all need to think about how to pursue it. Just wanted to give you a heads-up."

Tommy's head felt about full. He thanked Fred and followed June to her desk to go over his new salary, which was more generous than he expected, and sign documents. She told him she hoped to call him by the next day with a date and time for the senator's interview. He immediately felt worse. He was sure he wasn't ready, no matter how he prepared.

He met briefly with Vince, who seemed shocked Tommy was going to do an interview with the senator. It was clear from his body language and his terse responses to Tommy's questions that he thought the wrong person was picked to handle it. He wasn't very helpful.

Tommy needed to find Albright.

10
BAD DAY AND WORSE DAY

Tommy had planned to go to Denny's and talk to Albright first thing in the morning, but he overslept. He'd experienced a restless night and woke up with a pounding headache. Since it was too late to get to Denny's and still meet Captain Jefferson at nine, he opted for a bowl of cereal.

He pulled into the Sears parking lot right at nine and looked around, but didn't see a police car or any other vehicle with anyone waiting inside. He pulled farther into the lot, away from other cars, so he'd be visible. There was little traffic, so he was sure he could spot Jefferson driving in. After thirty minutes, he began to wonder if the man would show. Just as he was thinking of leaving, two patrol cars sped up to block his car, front and back, lights flashing.

This was not a clandestine meeting.

One officer got out quickly, unholstered his gun and crouched behind his car door. From the other car, another did the same. Tommy thought he might puke or, if he completely lost it, start screaming.

A senior-looking cop got out from behind the wheel of the second car. "Need you to put your hands out the window," he called out.

Tommy did as he was told. The other two ran up to his

car, one in front and pointing his gun at Tommy through the windshield. The other pulled open the passenger door.

"I don't have a gun. I'm a reporter for the *Journal*. What's going on here?" Tommy tried to sound forceful, but even to his own ears he sounded terrified.

"Just keep quiet, I'll ask the questions. What are you doing here?" shouted the older cop, who seemed to be in charge.

"I'm meeting someone. Why are you pointing guns at me?"

"I told you to shut the fuck up. You don't ask questions, got it?"

Tommy decided he'd better stay quiet. It seemed possible these guys might shoot him just because they were angry—but why?

Two more cars pulled up, each unmarked and filled to the brim with police, adding eight more to the situation, ensuring the hardened criminal mastermind Tommy Jacks could not escape. They huddled briefly before one of the new officers approached Tommy.

"You can put your hands back in. Can I see some ID?"

Tommy felt an almost overwhelming impulse to tell the official thug what he could do and where he could go, but his better judgment took hold. He gave the officer his license and business card. The officer nodded and handed them back. He went back to the huddle without a word, then returned.

"Sorry, Mister Jacks. Looks like we made a mistake. You're free to go." He started to walk away.

"Free to go?! *Free to fucking go?!* What the fuck are you talking about? You bastards were ready to shoot me. Now it's 'Oh, sorry, see ya later.' Bullshit! I want names and information."

The leader gave Tommy a dark look. "Goddamn reporters."

He got back in his car along with the rest of his posse, and they left.

Tommy sat, stunned. He got out, walked around the car several times, then threw his hands up in the air and yelled as loud as he could. "Shit!"

Louongo shrugged. "Could be you're just cursed, kid."

Tommy hadn't been able to track down Albright, and he had to tell someone what happened. He gave Louongo a dirty look. "Yeah, that's definitely a possibility. But why would so many cops show up at once? They knew I'd be there. This was not a casual thing."

"Well, you haven't told me why you were there. So, if I had to guess, I'd say you were there to meet someone on some kind of nosy reporter business. Maybe that person decided you were not his friend anymore and called the cops—claimed you were Jack the Ripper or something. But most likely, you were in the wrong place at the wrong time. You probably don't know this, but that parking lot is a known drug drop—lots of that going on there. So, you're sitting there, and maybe they were waiting on someone to pull in and drop something off and, wham! They jump all over you. Those two other unmarked cars sounded like the way vice cops operate—in packs."

"Jeez, that makes sense." Louongo was something of a lowlife, but he knew his stuff—lowlife stuff. "What can I do about it?"

"You mean, like sue the bastards? Or find out where they live and kidnap their children?" Louongo smiled. "You can't do shit. They violated all kinds of laws, so they should be arrested—oh wait, that would be the *cops* you'd have to contact to have the *cops* arrested. Could be a problem. My advice: forget about it. These cops are not your friendly movie cops who protect civilians. These guys are more like thugs than cops, and they're in a daily war. They're dangerous people. You don't want to start a fight with vice cops."

Tommy left Louongo's office thinking there was something seriously wrong with the whole messed-up world. Cops more dangerous than criminals attack an innocent guy just sitting in his car in a parking lot, and there's nothing he can do about it. Well, he could at least write about it. The thought made him feel a little better.

He was leaving downtown on Broadway when he realized he wasn't far from Hans Barbeque. Hans was in a poor, mostly black part of town on a short dirt road near the middle of the city. There had to be more zoning violations there than he could count. Nevertheless, it was only a short drive from the downtown high-rises, full of barbecue-loving white guys in suits. He could see the line stretching half a block. He loved the place almost as much as Del Rancho. He ordered a chopped brisket sandwich with extra sauce, and before he'd even paid, he was handed his order. He was able to forget about everything else for a few minutes.

He headed to the capitol press room and his favorite desk in the back to call June.

"Tommy, I'm so glad you called. We have a couple of times that will work for Knight, and I wanted to pin down a schedule." June went over the times the senator's office gave her, each in the next two days.

"Try to get the one two days out. I need time to get prepared. This still has me nervous." He felt like he was whining, but it was the truth.

"I know. Just try to relax. I think your best source for help is Albright. Have you talked to him?"

"Been tryin', haven't gotten him yet."

"He left a message this morning that he wanted to talk to you. No other details. He said to call him or meet him at Denny's tomorrow."

"Thanks." Tommy called his dad but got no answer. He called Tracy at work and was told she was out on an assignment. He didn't leave a message.

It hadn't been a good day. What Tommy needed was a pizza to go from Rizzo's and the comfort of his own bed.

Sammy House couldn't remember a time when he wasn't homeless. He acknowledged that was his choice, insofar as he had a choice. People offered to help him many times over the years, but usually they required him to be sober first. Sammy House didn't want to be sober.

His memory wasn't very good, but he was pretty sure he'd been drinking since he was a teenager, a long time ago. Sometimes it was whisky, sometimes cheap wine—whatever he could afford or get his hands on. Some years ago, he had discovered heroin. It was his greatest mistake. When he was just a drunk, there was never a day he did not want a drink. But if for some reason he couldn't find the money to buy a drink, he could survive and try again the next day. Heroin was a monster that never let you go, even for a day.

Heroin became his only purpose. He tried shoplifting, but homeless people are automatically considered suspicious. He was obviously homeless, so clerks would follow him. After a couple of arrests and some time in jail, he started stealing from cars. One of his pals taught him how to pop open locked car doors. It was surprising what people would leave in them. He had started begging on the streets in Chicago where people seemed concerned, even generous; but the weather forced him to move south. Oklahoma was less friendly and definitely less generous.

He sat with his back against a building across the street from the rescue mission, waiting for a free meal. He didn't feel well at all. He looked up and saw his skinny, annoying dealer crossing the street.

"You look like hell, Sammy. But cheer up. I got some great shit for you, free. It's new, and my guy says it's the best he's ever had—he's got me passing out samples. How 'bout it, Sammy? Wanna feel better?" Sammy felt the package being pressed into his hand. "Have fun, asshole."

Sammy hated his life. He hated the dealer. And he hated heroin. He should have stayed a drunk. That night, he used it. He didn't survive.

OK Journal

My View—Tommy Jacks

Let's agree that abuse of certain drugs can be a bad thing. Heroin, for example, is characterized by every dependable expert—including, and often especially, the people who use it—as instantly addictive and dangerous. It's a kind of morphine, and in some countries it's used as a palliative. That means it's given to people who are dying and in pain. It might even make them die quicker, but at least they won't suffer as much.

But it's completely illegal here. Partly because doctors prefer other, less addictive stuff that does the same job. Mostly, however, it's against the law because any amount of legal heroin could make life even harder for police and federal agents, whose hands are already full fighting the unrelenting tide of illegal drugs.

Illegal heroin is cheap to make, wins new customers every minute, and makes more money each year than everybody reading or writing this paper will see in our lives, combined. Preachers in their Sunday pulpits call it a tool of the devil, and chances are they're right. It takes a devil to talk people into throwing their lives away. And everyone who knows says the same thing: if you mess with the people who bring heroin into this country, your life is worth less than a junkie's.

Heroin isn't a matter of civil disagreement. The cops who stand between us and the drug trade, a source told me, "are in a daily war." In fact, this person told me on condition of anonymity, they can be just as grim and deadly as the criminal organizations that bring the devil's powder to our streets. They kind of have to be. If you want to fight a war, you have to confront your enemy where he is, with equal force and determination. And make no mistake, the vice squad of the Oklahoma City Police, just like federal officers and others involved, are up for the fight.

That all sounds stirring and inspiring, but we pay a price for it. It means the streets those police are sworn to protect are not particularly serene, let alone safe. An innocent agreement to meet someone in a remote place—the sort of thing reporters regularly have to do with their sources, because the truth isn't always just out there waiting to be picked like ripe peaches—can turn into a very hairy situation without warning.

Without going into too much detail, I'll just say I haven't had so many guns pointed at me since I played cowboys and Indians with the neighborhood kids. Yeah, that's worth a grin, and I can talk that way now. After all, you're not reading my obituary.

But if you're among the one or two who read this column more or less faithfully, you might notice that I somehow wind up getting police revolvers pointed at my nose a lot more often than is called for. And it's getting on my nerves.

Yes, we have to do something about a problem like heroin. But is "almost shoot first and bellow questions later but don't answer any" the best idea? And then, once a mistake is admitted, only say, "Oops. Wrong guy. Our mistake. Now, get out of here"?

If an innocent anybody has to die before somebody in power asks that question, something is terribly wrong. Everyone knows how far the police will go to protect the rights of someone who works for your right to know. And we know that's not far enough to bother with measuring. 🦃

11

BAD NEWS, GOOD NEWS

Fog and light mist made Tommy feel like he was driving through a tunnel from one safe haven—his apartment—to another—Denny's, Albright's favorite. He shuddered. Maybe he was just chilled. The cool, wet air was a nice change, if a sudden one. The parking lot was brimming, as on most mornings. Tommy had to park on a side street and walk through the mist.

He entered the restaurant, surprised to see a group at Albright's table. Joining his morning routine of newspapers and breakfast were Louongo and the two newly returned bodyguards. It was like a before and after picture for some male fashion magazine—the slobs, Albright and Louongo, were the before, and the impeccably dressed Max and Nathan were the after. Tommy didn't want a crowd—he wanted a private conversation with Albright—but even so, the scene struck him as comical.

"Good morning." Tommy addressed the group.

Several nods. No smiles. Tommy thought about leaving, but Albright spoke up, "You waiting on an invitation? Have a seat. Want breakfast?"

"No, just coffee." He signaled the waitress. "Is this a private meeting?"

Albright stared at Tommy a bit too long, then spoke. "This

is about you. You've got some problems, and we're here to figure out how to help. So, try to be civil."

"What kind of problems?" He scoffed. Still, he was curious.

"As best we can determine, that Captain Jefferson guy
doesn't exist. There is no Jefferson in the traffic division. The
only Jefferson in the police department is a Mike Jefferson,
who works in the carpool. He's in his sixties. So, he's not your
guy. The 'Jefferson' you met was part of a setup. Your encounter
with the vice cops was also a setup. They were hassling you.
There was no mistaken identity, or that's what we think. They
were intentionally going after you."

"Why? What's this about?"

"Chief Underwood would be the logical guess. You've made
an enemy out of him with your columns. So, we think he's
pushing back. Why they didn't stick with trying to trick you
into some kind of false claim against the chief and demand
you be fired, we don't know. Could be the chief became aware
of *our* digging, and it spooked him. At that point, he decided
to send in the troops to scare you. There's no question he sees
you as a threat, and he won't stop as long as he thinks that. The
first step was to scare you with a goon squad. The next might
be to kill you." Albright seemed solemn. So did everyone else.

"Kill me? The police chief might kill me? That can't be true."

"You can say clever, cutesy things in your column about the
chief's lifestyle, but he knows perfectly well what he does to
support that lifestyle. Now he thinks maybe *you* know, too.
He's not cute or clever. He's a thug with a badge, backed up by
a whole police department. He'll defend his power, and he'll
do it in ugly, direct ways. No letters to the editor. He'll attack
with guns blazing."

Tommy felt stunned. Somebody might want him dead because of something he'd written? And that somebody was the police chief? "What should I do?"

"You have options. The first, and you should consider this very seriously, is that you quit. You sure as hell didn't hire on for a life-and-death battle against real people with real guns. Bill Anderson doesn't want you dead. This changes everything. And if you tell them what's going on, they'll stop you from writing, at least in the paper. They'd stop you because that would be the only way to make sure you don't get killed for doing your job. They'd never be able to live with that. It's one thing to write about corrupt politicians. Some of those idiots might be dangerous, but it's not likely lethal. This is tangling with a dangerous man who has, in effect, his own private army. I'm sure quitting would be Bill and Fred's advice, and it's mine. Go on a vacation to Florida and lie in the sun. If your dad finds out about this, he'll hit the ceiling. He'll insist that Bill fire you. You don't have any duty to risk your life to try to fix society's problems."

Tommy knew Albright was right. His pay, even after the raise, wasn't much more than he could make waiting tables full time, and sure not worth risking his life for. But he hadn't become a journalist for the money. He'd done it because he *wanted* to fix society's problems. Okay, he'd never thought about risking his life, but it *was* what he wanted to do. Could he really run away and hide, and somehow be the same person who dreamed of changing the world?

"Other options?"

"All involve risk. I can talk to Bill about hiring some protection." He glanced at Max and Nathan.

Max spoke up. "Protection has limits. I can tell you no matter who is hired to protect someone, there's always a way to get to that person if the other side really wants to and is patient. Protection can never be one hundred percent."

Back to Albright. "Another option is that we can take an aggressive legal strategy. We could file for a restraining order against the chief and the entire police force."

Louongo jumped in. "I like that shit a lot. We can get a lot of press, even get a hearing. It'll drive the chief nuts. Then, if they even harm a hair on your head, the FBI's here in a New York minute to take a hard look at the chief and his goons. Of course, the restraining order will be denied, but we get great protection just out of the publicity."

"There's a downside, though," Albright put in, "That's *also* the publicity. It's not going to sit well with Bill Anderson. And there might be some lingering effects on you and your career, but it has the dual benefit of offering you some protection, even if it's not ironclad, and it exposes the chief to public scrutiny." Everyone else at the table nodded. "Another approach is that we go see the feds, lay out what we know, and see if they'll start an investigation on the police chief and offer you protection. The problem there seems to be that no one at this table trusts the FBI any more than they trust the chief."

Tommy spoke too loudly because he was scared. "I'm not comfortable with any of this. I don't want to quit. I also don't want protection. And the publicity angle might cause the *Journal* to fire me anyway. I need to think about what makes sense."

"Don't yell at me," Albright said. "What you *need* to do is talk to your dad. He has to know what's happening, and I think he can help you decide the best way to go. Give him a call."

When Tommy was young, his dad ignored him, often for weeks. Oh, he'd be around for a few meals here and there, bring home groceries and give Tommy pocket money. But he was never really *there.* Ray went through a horrible period of grief after Tommy's mother died only a few months after her diagnosis of breast cancer. Ray became a drunk and ignored everything and everyone, living for years in a whisky fog. He married the wrong people and left them quickly, or they left him. But after prison, he was a different man, trying to be a better father. Tommy very much wanted his advice.

Tommy's head felt like it might explode. How could so much crap happen so fast? Talking to his dad was the best way to get his thoughts straight. He needed a sense of order and direction; and needed it now. He decided he'd go to Tracy's house and wait. It would be several hours before either of them were home. His apartment was on the way so he was going to stop there first. He needed a quiet place to gather his thoughts.

Tommy's habit was to throw any mail onto the overcrowded table in the corner, but today he needed a distraction so he thumbed through the stack. He was expecting the bills and advertisements, but not the letter from Alexander's office—more specifically, from Patsy White. She wanted him to call as soon as he could so that she could finalize arrangements for him to give a deposition regarding the Douglas matter.

Tommy called.

"Law office of Lawrence Alexander, how may I help you?"

He fell immediately under the spell of her voice. "Hi, it's Tommy Jacks. Just got your letter. Sorry if this is late, but I don't always check my mail."

"That's okay, Tommy. I called, but never seemed to get you, so I sent a letter. Just want to get you scheduled for next week to meet with Mister Alexander and a court stenographer." She offered a couple of dates and times; Tommy picked one. "Thanks, all done. How're you doing?"

Tommy hesitated. The question sounded personal. Maybe he was just daydreaming. "Well, it's actually been kind of a tough few days. Seems like it must be my month to stir up all kinds of trouble."

The soothing voice said, "I'm so sorry. Maybe we should meet for a drink tonight and have dinner, and you could tell me all about it."

Tommy nearly dropped the phone. Did she really just ask him out? "Sure, um, that sounds great. Where would you like to meet?"

"I live near the capitol, so how about someplace in that neighborhood?"

"What about Risso's?"

"That's perfect. I love their pizzas." They set a time to meet.

He had to sit a moment to absorb what happened. He had just made a date with the most beautiful woman on the planet. Maybe things were looking up.

He was sure he would be at Tracy's before anyone was there, but he couldn't wait any longer. His mind was racing with thoughts of the dangerous position he was in and the prospect of dinner with Pasty. One bad, one good. Tracy's covered front porch had a comfortable cushioned bench that would be perfect for a short nap. Just what he needed.

"Tommy? Tommy, is everything okay?" It was Tracy, shaking him awake.

Tommy stirred. "Oh, sure. Everything's fine. I was headed home and thought I'd stop by and say hi."

"Great, come on in." She unlocked the front door. "Not sure when your dad'll be here, but it shouldn't be long." She went about dropping bags around the house, all the time looking quite serious. "Wish I'd've known you were coming by. I could've made some dinner. Your dad's dinner preferences seem to run toward sandwiches and chips—not something a young lady can eat every night and keep her girlish figure." She seemed to force a smile.

"Yeah, I don't think anyone would accuse my dad of being a gourmet eater. You seem upset. Is something wrong?"

"Oh, Tommy," she sighed. "I think there is. I haven't been able to talk to your dad about it, so keep this between us until I can, okay? I was fired today."

"Fired? You're kidding. Why would they fire you? You're the best."

"Well, thanks." She smiled warmly. "But the reality in the TV business is, unless you're an anchor, they only want young, attractive women."

"You're the most beautiful woman on TV. That doesn't make any sense."

Tracy walked over and gave Tommy a kiss on the cheek. "Thank you. But the truth is, I'm getting a little too old for field reporting. If I hadn't been so reckless, I'd probably be anchor by now, and it wouldn't matter. But I'm just extra payroll. So, *adios.*"

"I bet you have another job by next week."

"I don't know. I've worked for half the stations in this market by now, and they all work off of the same script, as far as a woman's age goes. So, it's going to be tough. Your dad's going to take this real hard. It seemed like we were just getting everything together. Us living together was going just perfect. We had extra cash every month. Now, this."

They hadn't been paying attention, so they jumped when Tommy's dad came in. "Hey, what are you two conspiring about?" Ray seemed in a great mood.

"Tommy's coming over Sunday for dinner. We're going to have a pot roast, and I'm going to completely humiliate him at Monopoly."

"That's fantastic. Always good to have a Monopoly victim other than me. How are you, son?" Ray gave Tommy a big hug.

"Oh, you know, a few problems here and there. I think on Sunday I'd like to talk to you about some of the things that are happening."

"Of course. I'll look forward to it."

Tommy hesitated a bit, but quickly decided he should leave and let Tracy break her news—it was the right thing to do. "Well, guess I'd better be going. I have a date tonight, if you can believe that."

Tracy was immediately on alert. "A date? With whom? Do I know her? How did you meet her?"

"She's Larry Alexander's assistant. I'll tell you all about it Sunday. Gotta run."

He left them at the door, smiling about his own news, knowing the smiles wouldn't last long.

12
DATE NIGHTMARE

Tommy felt better after a quick shower and a change of clothes. Leaving for Rizzo's now meant he would be a bit early, but he was too anxious to just sit at home. He had more to think about than he could handle. Tracy's news had complicated his plan to unload his personal problems on his dad. He'd wanted to talk to his dad about the madness with the chief, but with Tracy's news the timing wasn't right. After great and serious thought, he took the path chosen by millions—ignore it. *Hell, who knows? Maybe it'll all just magically go away.*

Risso's lot was almost full, so he parked at the far end. Larry would be in a good mood, at least. Larry wasn't at the front when Tommy arrived. Probably in the back causing havoc with his cooks. He considered ordering a drink but didn't want to appear too anxious when his date arrived. He was still trying to get his head around Patsy asking him out. He took a seat in the waiting area just as Larry emerged from the back.

"Hey, Tommy. What's goin' on? Need a pizza to go?" The smile on Larry's face was always in proportion to the amount of business he was experiencing, and tonight he was beaming.

"No, I'm waiting on someone. We're going to eat."

Larry looked down at the seating chart. "Goin' be tough to get you in for probably thirty minutes or so. Will that be okay?"

"Oh, sure. She isn't even here yet."

"You can wait in the bar. Tell me what she looks like and I'll show her in."

"She's about five-foot-five, with blonde hair and blue eyes. Very pretty. Her name's Patsy." Tommy blushed, maybe because of the grin on Larry's face.

"No problem." The grin got bigger.

Tommy found a booth in the back and ordered a beer. He still couldn't quite decide if he liked alcohol. Mixed drinks never seemed to taste right to him. He felt his hesitation was based on experience with his dad, but he wasn't interested in thinking about that tonight. He took a sip. It tasted pretty good. He relaxed.

A few minutes later he looked up to see Larry walking toward him, smiling. Right behind him walked Patsy White. Tommy slid out of the booth and stood, noticing all the admiring eyes following her. The office Patsy was amazing, but this on-a-date Patsy was stunning.

She walked right up; gave him a hug and a kiss on the cheek. He knew she was flirting and having fun, which was just fine by him.

"You look fantastic. I think I should have dressed up more."

"You're fine. I was just in a mood to spark up a little. Is that okay?"

Tommy nodded vigorously. She ordered a beer and he got another.

"I just love this place," she chuckled. "I've been in a couple of times for lunch. I hear it's been here forever."

"Risso's has been a favorite of politicians mostly because it's so close by the capitol. You mix politics with booze, and you're bound to get some excitement. My dad came here a lot. I think the first food I remember was Risso's pizza, usually cold."

"I've met your dad. He's been in to meet with Mister Alexander. He seems real nice."

Tommy was thinking he could listen to her read the phone book and be thrilled. "Yeah, my dad's nice. We've had kind of a hard time, but things are great with us right now. Tell me, how did you end up working in a law office?"

Patsy smiled, clearly noticing he'd changed subjects. "True confession time. My dad is Uncle Larry's brother." She giggled a little. "So, the honest answer is he hired me because I couldn't find a job, and he owed my dad a favor."

Tommy chuckled. "Well, it's good to hear all your hard work in law school paid off."

"Nope. Never went to law school. I really don't do any legal work anyway. Uncle Larry calls me his assistant, but it's really more like 'flunky.' His real assistant, Mrs. Roberts, does all the legal stuff. My jobs are mostly to answer the phone, get the mail, make coffee, and do whatever else they tell me to do. You're the impressive one—you have your own column in the newspaper, and you're so young. How'd that happen?"

"Well, I had a little daddy help myself." Not only was she beautiful, she was witty and smart—and easy to talk to. "You probably know he was the chairman of the state Democratic Party, and he talked Bill Anderson, the owner of the paper, into running for governor. And he and my dad became friends."

"Family connections always help. We've only been in Oklahoma about a year, so we weren't around for that election. But I've heard stories."

"How did you end up here?"

"My dad took a job with Kerr-McGee as their in-house legal counsel. He's something of an expert in oil and gas law, and this was a super opportunity for him. So we moved here from California."

"That's a big change. Where in California?"

"Los Angeles."

"I'm surprised you left. You could have been a movie star." Tommy immediately felt stupid for saying it, but it was what popped into his head.

"I have no idea how many attractive women are in L.A. trying to be movie stars, but it could be a billion. They're everywhere, in every lousy job there is. I never wanted anything to do with the movie business." She shrugged. "But moving from California was hard for me. I was old enough, I could have stayed on my own, but my parents are just so important to me. I couldn't imagine not having them close. I'm sure one of these days, when I've got them all settled in and I don't have to worry about them, I'll head back to L.A."

"I know what you mean. My dad's living with someone who's about as close to a mom as I've ever had, and it's great to have them together right here in town." Tommy thought about Tracy possibly having to move now that she'd lost her job. He felt a twinge of anxiety.

"Tracy Clark?"

Tommy smiled broadly. "That's right. How did you know?"

"You may not think about it too much, but you've been in the paper quite a bit. Especially when that girl was killed by the police. The reports mentioned you and her by name. Anyway, I've also asked my uncle about you, so maybe I know a lot." She gave him a sly grin.

Tommy leaned back a little. She'd been checking up on him. Good or bad? Good—had to be good. Patsy White was interested in him. He wanted to jump up and down and shout. Instead he just smiled.

"What are you grinning about?"

"Just feeling pretty happy."

Later they walked out to her car near the front door. Her car was much nicer than his. "I'd like to see you again," he volunteered. "Maybe tomorrow?"

She laughed, reached up, and gave him a kiss. "Let's give it a couple of days, and then you call me. I want to see you again, too." She winked, got in her car and drove off.

Tommy stood in the dark parking lot, relishing how great he felt until he noticed movement— headed toward him. He shook off the slight flicker of fear and started walking.

A man moved into his path. "This is a dangerous part of town, Tommy Asshole Jacks. People get hurt out here all the time. You really shouldn't be by yourself."

Tommy's fear rose fully. He sensed someone behind him and turned to see another man holding some kind of club. Hoping this would all go away didn't work. "You from Underwood?"

"Oh, no. We're just some common criminals attacking weak and helpless assholes like you." The guy in front was holding something, too—maybe a sap. He started toward Tommy. *What the hell is he going to do? Do I run? Will they shoot me if I do?* Tommy suspected these guys were pros at giving a beating and had no idea how to stop them. His only chance was to run, and he was about to when the man in front of him went down, face-first, onto the pavement.

In the next instant, Tommy heard blows being dealt and cracking bones behind him. He turned. The man with the club was down and out. Max stood over him, smiling. Over the other stood Nathan. As usual, he wasn't as expressive.

"Shit, shit, shit. My god. Where'd you guys come from? Shit! Are they dead?"

Max shook his head. "They'll live. We'll clean this up. You need to go home. And lock your doors. Until you decide what you're going to do—quit, sue the chief, whatever—we'll be around. No more trouble tonight. Go get some rest."

Tommy realized he'd made up his mind what to do. He wanted Louongo to run every legal maneuver he could, no holds barred. If Anderson didn't like it, then Tommy would quit. He wasn't going to live in fear. On the way home, he realized he was driving a little fast. He'd been scared out of his mind more often in the past few months than his entire life. Things had to change. He was a muckraker, which meant he was going to keep attacking everything that was wrong in the world. And he refused to live in fear anymore. He hated that he'd been so afraid, even if it was natural.

He needed power on his side. He wanted to be able to hire Max and Nathan so he'd be free to really go after people who deserved it. That felt better. He wasn't sure exactly how his decision would play out, but he sure as hell wasn't going to hide in the shadows. Bring it on, assholes.

13
TRUTH SEEKER OR NOT

The next morning, Tommy felt far less confident of what to do about Underwood. The "bring it on, assholes" idea seemed risky and childish. By habit, he was vulnerable to self-doubt during the first few moments of the day when his thoughts focused on his weaknesses. It became clear he needed advice, and the only person he really trusted was his dad.

At the capitol he found the closet-sized office of T.D. Mc-Fadden. The door was locked. He knocked, but no one answered, so he headed back to the lobby to find a pay phone and call McFadden's business office. He spotted his dad at the coffee shop talking to a couple of men. He hesitated, but Ray saw him and left the table at once.

"Hey, what luck. Got time for coffee?" Tommy was surprised to see his dad so happy. Had Tracy not told him she'd lost her job?

"Sure. I was just looking for you." Tommy knew he didn't sound happy.

"What's wrong?"

"It's a problem I seem to have with the police chief."

On a bench tucked into a quiet corner of the lobby, he told his dad everything, including the incident the night before. He explained Albright's options and his feelings about them.

Ray thought a moment. "There's no question Bill doesn't want you to get killed. My concern is, it may be too late to quit. Even if you do, Underwood still might want revenge. The threat to him has to be coming from more than just you. But as long as he thinks you're part of it, he'll keep going at you. We need Bill to hit the chief with an editorial. But even more important, we have to get the *Sun* and Robbie Gilmore to go after Underwood. Then you become a minor problem to him."

"Doesn't Gilmore support Underwood?"

Ray shook his head. "I don't think so. Not that I've talked to Robbie about it, but I doubt he's a fan of the chief. He's too outlandish, too pompous—not Robbie's style. We need to get him to focus on Underwood's dark side."

"Can you get him to do that?"

"I can try. I know he'll see me. First, we need to make sure Albright's bodyguards are still on duty. You need protection. Second, you need to see Bill, tell him what's happened and what you think should be done—the legal proceeding and the publicity. If he says no and forbids you from writing about this, then I think you have to quit. We'll make a new plan if that happens. My gut tells me Bill won't do that, though, and that he'll support you with the paper and with money."

"Thanks, Dad." He appreciated his dad's support, but likely enjoyed his approval even more. "Another thing that's happened is that I'm supposed to interview Senator Knight one-on-one and write a feature story. I'm really nervous about it. I'm not sure I'm ready for that. I told Fred, but he insists it'll be good for me and for the paper. Can you help me figure out how I should approach this?"

"Wow, I'm surprised Fred would toss you into that fire-pit.

Knight's an ornery old fart, and he won't be patient with a novice. This may seem funny to you, but the way to approach this is to think of Knight as if he was Albright. They're different, but they have a lot in common. The most important thing is that you can't show fear. If either of those guys sense fear, they attack. One big difference is that Albright is essentially a decent human being. Knight isn't. His ego's gigantic. As far he's concerned, no one except himself knows anything that matters. He and I butted heads over everything."

"That doesn't sound promising. What should I ask him?"

"Like most people, he likes to talk about himself—just more so. But I'd stay away from politics. You bring up some of the stuff he's supported, he'll think you are being critical. I've never met anyone so sensitive to criticism, real or imagined. I think it has to do with the fact that much of what he supports in Washington isn't what his constituents actually want. He's survived mostly by hiding what he thinks and what bills he supports. And his weird lifestyle is off limits. Not only would he cut the interview short, but the paper wouldn't print most of the facts if they came out. I can tell you more about that, but it doesn't matter right now."

"Albright hinted he was a womanizer, or maybe even chased men. Any of that true?"

"It's not anything I could prove, but most people in Washington know about his cheating on his wife. The man-chasing sounds like a rumor started by people who hate him—and there are a lot of them. Some people can handle power with grace. Knight can't. He's a bully."

"Hard to believe he can get re-elected."

"Yep, until you realize he's sucked up to the Gilmores for

years. If J.H. Gilmore needed a favor out of Washington, Knight was right there. He's represented the Gilmores and not necessarily the people, and the Gilmores have rewarded him for that."

"So, why does Bill Anderson want this feature? Doesn't sound like Knight's his kind of politician."

"Good question. They're pretty much exact opposites, that's for sure. My guess, it's just business. He thinks it'll be good for the paper. Most of Bill's decisions over the last year or so have been to keep the paper from folding. Anything that might boost circulation will seem like the thing to do. The Bill Anderson I knew would've been more likely to run a hit piece on Knight, not a feature story. But he's under a lot of pressure. So, like most of us, he adapts."

Their talk left Tommy less sure whether the whole Knight interview was a good idea. He was a lot more comfortable with the idea of a hit piece.

"I'll get an appointment with Robbie," Ray told him, getting up to leave. "Anything big happens, I'll give you a call."

Tommy headed to the press room to put in some typewriter time. He was daydreaming about Patsy when in walked Albright, unexpected and unannounced. He was, as usual, abrupt and to the point.

"Heard about last night. We need to implement something before you get killed. Have you talked to your dad or Anderson? We need a decision on what to do, now."

"I've talked to my dad, but not Bill. I'm going to try to see him this afternoon. But it doesn't matter about him. He'll either support my decision or not. I want Louongo to go after the restraining order. I'll figure out a way to pay him. My dad's going to see Robbie Gilmore to see if he'll help expose Underwood, put pressure on him. I want Max and Nathan to stick around, but I'm not sure I can get the money to pay them. And I'd love it if you'd blast Underwood in *The Banner*." Tommy listed the elements of strategy with firm conviction, if only in voice.

"Don't worry about the bodyguards. They're in town visiting me, and they need things to do or they'll get bored. As far as Louongo, I can't speak for him. But he's cheap. If you like, I can talk to Bill after you do if there's any problem with him. For now, I'll make contact with Louongo. Keep me up to date." Albright turned to leave.

"How'd you get here?"

"Stupid bus comes right to the capitol. Zero people riding the damned thing, but a great schedule if you want to go from downtown to here. Must be some kind of political thing. Your self-absorbed government in action. See ya."

Tommy drove to the *Journal*. He wasn't looking forward to talking with Anderson. He was his boss after all, and a friend of both his dad and Albright. He chatted with June about scheduling and the Knight interview, telling her he was ready and looking forward to it. That was all lies.

Anderson greeted Tommy warmly. "Glad you asked to see me. I was just thinking I should talk to you a little about this Knight thing and make sure you're comfortable with it. But first, tell me what's on your mind."

Everyone always said what a nice man Bill Anderson was. Tommy hadn't been around him that much, but as far as he'd seen, it seemed true. He relaxed as much as he could. "I have a problem with Chief Underwood. It's possible, although I can't prove it, he's trying to kill me." Tommy paused.

Anderson's eyes popped wide. "What! Trying to kill you? Why do you think so?"

Tommy laid out the story, sparing no detail, starting with the first time he heard rumors about Underwood and the first references he'd put in his column. He finished with the "Captain Jefferson" matter and a sanitized version of the incident at Risso's, replacing Max and Nathan with helpful, if rough and ready, strangers. He talked about Albright and his dad to add credibility to his story.

Anderson looked worried and in deep thought. He looked up. "I can't tell you how badly that makes me feel. We've pushed you very fast and allowed you to take chances, mostly because I wanted to increase circulation. I never once thought it might create problems like these. I'm sorry, Tommy. I should've thought this through. I'm not sure what to do."

Tommy felt sorry for him. "It's not your fault, Mister Anderson. If it's anyone's fault, it's mine. But the bad guy here is Underwood. Not us." He went on, giving him a complete outline of what he, his dad, and Albright had discussed, including talking to Robbie Gilmore.

Anderson chuckled dryly. "Wouldn't that be ironic—teaming up with the *Sun* to attack corruption. I know J.H. wouldn't do it, but maybe Robbie really is different. All this sounds well thought out, and of course I trust your dad and Taylor. I just wish we had more conclusive proof about the chief. I've heard the stories, and his expensive ways sure suggest something, but we don't have any witnesses or documents."

"What we have," Tommy answered, "is an increase in crime statistics and what appears to be a surge in illegal drugs. That's documented by the feds. I don't know how responsible Underwood is for that, but it gives us a way to be critical without accusing him of taking bribes."

Anderson nodded. "Okay Tommy. I'm on board. I want to consult with our legal people, and I want to go over things with Fred, but you have my approval. We need to be really cautious about accuracy on this one. I want Fred involved in every review and edit. And tell your dad, if something works out with Robbie, I'd like him to set up a meeting for me with him, too. Also, you need to get an estimate on the legal costs and let me approve it. The paper will pay," he chuckled, "but I'm not giving Joe Louongo a blank check."

"I can take care of that, all of it. I appreciate your support."

Anderson changed subjects. "Now, about this Knight deal. I never told Fred you should go in with kid gloves, but I don't want a war. Somewhere in the middle is an interesting interview. Try not to annoy the old fool—which mostly means don't bring up his faults—but see if you can get him on the record on things that are important to our readers. He's our representative in the U.S. Senate. What we need to know about are the measures he plans to support or oppose. It may be hard, but try to get him to be specific. I'm sure you think this is too soon for you to handle something like this, but I think you'll do just fine."

OK Journal

My View—Tommy Jacks

I've been told to quit by just about everybody except the people who could tell me that and make it stick—meaning the people who sign my paycheck. I've been threatened with far worse than the loss of a job, too. And if you've been keeping score at home, you know I haven't even been on my beat for all that long.

Still, it's amazing how much experience has come with the territory in so short a time. "Experience," the writer C.S. Lewis once sighed, "that most brutal of teachers. But you learn. My God, do you learn."

Yep. I learned. I learned what I'm made of. After dodging bullets—real ones, understand—and nearly being arrested for asking questions that anyone else in the world would only get a straight answer for, and getting slammed into a wall just for doing my job, I've figured myself out. Here's what I've learned, as a kind of inventory.

I don't own a gun—can't afford one, and wouldn't carry it around anyway—but I've had one pointed at me at least twice

that I know of, and that's only this year.

Although I am not a self-styled hero or some wild-eyed reporter with a death wish, I've never tucked tail and ran.

And I'm not alone. I have a lot of people I depend on and who depend on me, spread all over this city. Some you may know. Some you'll never know or see, no matter how hard you look.

Put that together and you have an imperfect, unarmed, unheroic guy who, like a growing number of others, is nonetheless fed up with an attitude held by certain people in this town, to wit: that everyone should kneel before the powerful, and their corruption, bullying, and lies, even if that would make life easier.

Nope. Can't do it. I'm not saying I'm the guy who can turn things around for everybody next week. I'm saying all the things that have been done to try to entrap or intimidate this reporter have backfired. Brutal as the experience has been, I learned. My God, did I learn. 🦔

14

SOMETHING OLD AND SOMETHING BLUE

Ray Jacks called the *Oklahoma Sun* to speak to Robbie Gilmore. He was transferred to Gilmore's secretary's assistant, to whom he repeated his request. Her questions were simple; who he was and why he wanted to talk to Mister Gilmore. He patiently explained that he was an old friend and wished the subject to remain private. She huffed, but put him through to Gilmore's secretary, who asked him again who he was and why he wanted to talk to Gilmore. By now Ray was losing patience, yet he explained again that he was an old friend of Robbie's and the matter was private. The secretary put him on hold without comment.

"My goodness, a voice from the past. How are you, Ray?" The first friendly voice he heard belonged to Robert J. "Robbie" Gilmore, childhood friend and adulthood enemy.

"Hello, Robbie. Heard about your dad; so sorry. How is he?"

"Not good. He really isn't with us anymore. He's just being kept alive. It's sad." Robbie paused a second. "What can I do for you, Ray?"

"I'd like to meet and talk about some things. They're related to my son and to Chief Underwood. I think it's best if we talk in person."

Again, Robbie paused. "That was a real tragedy for your son when Judy Jackson was killed. How's he holding up?"

"I think he's okay. He's had a lot to deal with, mostly thanks to me, but I think he's handling everything pretty well. I really want to talk about Underwood. Shouldn't take long." Ray wanted to end the conversation before he said something along the lines of "Life has been hell ever since you put me in prison." That wouldn't lead to the discussion he wanted.

"Okay. How about this afternoon or first thing in the morning?" Robbie still sounded friendly.

"Morning would be best for me—say, about nine in your office?"

"Sounds good, Ray. See ya then."

A lifetime had gone by since they'd last met face to face, but it would happen. Still, it seemed there should be more hoopla or something. "See ya," sounded too casual. Ray felt nervous about everything—his son, his job, his life with Tracy, money—and now he faced possible reconciliation with a best friend from the distant past. It was a lot to absorb.

Tommy had a heavy schedule of hearings at the capitol, and that felt good. For what seemed like years he'd been under stress, and the hearings were a comfort. All he had to do was sit back and listen. He'd come to view the system as something of a charade. Hearings were held about almost everything. Their results were largely ignored because bills were written behind closed doors, but the mundane folly of the whole exercise felt like an old bathrobe. You wouldn't want anyone to see you in it, but it was pleasant and familiar.

He deliberately took a seat next to Mike Sanders of the *Sun*, who regarded him with alarm and moved a couple of rows away. Probably for childish reasons, that also made Tommy feel good. The hearing started.

"The star columnist actually attending a legislative hearing. Slumming?" Vince smiled, but it sounded like a dig.

"I've been so damn busy I have to go to these hearings just to get some rest. What about you, Mr. Star-Front-Page-Reporter?' Can't be anything worth your time going on here."

"I don't know. Sometimes I think Fred sends me to these things just to get me out of the office. A reporter sitting at his desk reading the paper looks a little annoying if you're the guy paying him." They chuckled. It sounded like Fred.

"Anything happening with that Tinker body?"

"Not that I hear. They put Chuck on it. He got a bunch of inside info, but nothing we can print. I'm not sure if he's still on it. Something I'm hearing a lot about, which could be tied into it, is deaths due to drugs. Rumor has it that a heroin much stronger than usual is being sold on the street, and it's killing some users—and the cops are keeping it quiet."

That interested Tommy. "Got any proof?"

"You sound just like Fred. No. But I'm getting that from sources connected to the police and the coroner's office. If we could get enough data, I think it'll show that. But of course, the data's controlled by the police department."

"There any chance those drugs could have anything to do with Janet Knight's death?"

"Kinda doubt it. She sure as hell wasn't some street addict. If it was an overdose, it would have been on legal drugs prescribed by her personal drug pusher, that Doctor What's-His-Name."

"Yeah, I guess you're right. Did they ever issue a statement about her cause of death?"

"Not a peep. I've asked. They told me to go to hell, in a polite way."

"Why?"

"Just guessing, but I'd say the coroner doesn't agree it was an overdose—thinks it was something else, and that's a problem. Otherwise, why not just say, 'drug overdose,' and be done with it?"

"You know; I still have that interview with Knight in a couple of days. I know you're pissed about that. Can't blame you. You'd do a better job than I would. I know that, and I'm sure Bill and Fred know it. For whatever reason, they think my column adds to the circulation they want, so getting me on the front page with a feature story will build my image. I don't agree. And I don't want you mad at me."

"Well, yeah, I guess it did piss me off at first. But I'm over it. I know those guys are focusing more on short-term circulation numbers than anything else. Hell, I read your column like everyone else, so I know it's a hit. No worries. If you need me to help, just ask."

"Thanks." They shook hands with a smile. "That was one of my questions. How should I handle asking him about his wife's death?"

"Well, based on the shit I'm hearing, just come out and ask him if he did it." Chuckles from both of them, but Tommy still felt nervous about it.

The next hearing included Mitch Douglas. Tommy worried he might make another obscene gesture at him and ruin the atmosphere, but Douglas chose to ignore him. On one occasion he looked right at him but seemed to pretend not to see him. Being ignored by Douglas was a good thing.

After the final hearing of the day, Tommy headed to the press room. He wrote and made notes about the various matters debated and thought about Vince's ideas for questions to pose to Knight and what he'd said about the heroin. He couldn't get a firm handle on the scene. Sometimes you just had to wait until the other shoe dropped.

Oklahoma City had one of the oldest jazz clubs in the country in an industrial section just east of downtown. It once was called The Hole, when on most nights it featured Billy Marsh, a blues legend. People came from all over to hear Billy sing about life's miseries. People said if you could sit through one of his sets without crying, you weren't human. Because of Billy, The Hole attracted some of the best jazz players and blues singers of the time. Muddy Waters, John Lee Hooker, and Buddy Guy performed there. It was even rumored that Louis Armstrong and Charles Mingus dropped in for jam sessions.

The Hole wasn't swanky and existed for one reason—music. Its audiences were an odd mix of races and classes. The music had a real hold on them. Behind the scenes lurked another addiction—drugs. Police raided The Hole regularly. But the music went on.

One night, Billy Marsh was feeling little pain, but his music sounded particularly soulful. The crowd was enthralled. That night he collapsed onstage and died. The year was 1948, and people said Billy was maybe thirty-seven or thirty-eight. He died of a drug overdose, escaping the pain of his troubled life. The owner of The Hole was devastated. He renamed the club Billy's and mourned for weeks.

Performing at Billy's was a rite of passage for up-and-coming blues singers. They traveled from far and wide to make connections with singers and musicians of the past. Billy's added bathrooms to meet code requirements, but it remained basically a dump. Still, the crowds came for the music. On one night, a new singer named Tina Duncan performed. She was young but had built a good reputation on years of singing in Alabama and North Florida. People said there was something about her that reminded them of the old singers, that she had an old soul. She also was a heroin addict.

Her first set went over well. She was a perfectionist, however, and wasn't pleased, especially in a famous place like Billy's. She knew all about the people who sang and played there, and the tragic stories of their lives. Sometimes she cried by herself, dwelling on the pain so many suffered because they weren't accepted for who they were. She felt that rejection. During her break she consoled herself with heroin.

The crowd grew anxious when Tina was late to come back on. When she did appear, she was given a standing ovation—she was a hit. Tina gave the audience one of her best tearful performances. At the end of the set, she collapsed. People rushed to the stage, but she was dead. Drugs were killing the blues, one by one.

15
JUSTICE FOR NONE

It was an odd feeling, entering the impressive lobby of the *Oklahoma Sun*. Ray had seen and heard about it all his life, but never had been inside. It was a place that foisted evil upon the world—or at least, upon Ray. As childhood friends, he and Robbie Gilmore grew up in a swank neighborhood, but when life turned bleak for the Jacks family, all the Gilmores shunned them. The pain still lived inside Ray.

Of course, there was the more recent trauma when the Gilmores conspired with Ray's most recent ex-wife and spent effort and money to put Ray in prison on trumped-up charges of corruption. And now he entered the house of evil to ask for help. It was the right thing to do, but it didn't feel like it.

The receptionist in the lobby seemed friendly and asked him to wait while she called upstairs. The guard standing behind her seemed less so, taking a hard look at Ray even while he followed him to the elevators and held the door open. Ray wouldn't have been surprised if the guard had joined him in order to keep an eye on him. But he didn't.

If this was the lair of evil, it was well-appointed with old-money luxury—not garish, but established, durable, and opulent. Ray had been in luxury hotels with the same sumptuous atmosphere, places where ordinary folk didn't belong. He was a little embarrassed that he felt so impressed.

"Mister Jacks, welcome. Mister Gilmore will be with you in just a few minutes. May I get you something to drink—coffee, water?" She had to be the assistant to the secretary. She was studious-looking and subdued.

"No, thanks. I'm fine." Ray took a seat on the leather sofa.

"Ray. My goodness, Ray. It has been so long. We should have done this ages ago. Please, come in." Robbie could not have been more welcoming. Anyone watching would believe he was greeting a close friend he hadn't seen in years.

He took Ray to a small table in a corner of his lavish office. "Before we start, I have something I need to say," he began. "What we did to you was totally wrong. I still can't believe I participated in that. I never wanted to hurt you or your family. Something happened with my father. He more or less lost his mind, and I guess I lost my own for a while. It seemed everything was 'us versus them.' My father got more and more paranoid about everything and everyone. During those last years, I don't think he even trusted me. I lost my sense of right and wrong. I wish I could say it was all J.H. and I tried to stop him, but that isn't the truth. I was caught up in the battle just like he was, and we both had that war mentality. All I can do now is apologize and offer you any help that I can give."

Being in prison for four years had been life-crushing. It almost destroyed Ray and left him a stranger to his own son. Robbie's apology was the most absurd thing he'd ever heard. *Oh, sorry about those hundreds of insults and threats you had to live through . . . sorry about more than a thousand days and nights with no privacy or security, filled with terror . . . sorry about not seeing your son for years and making him hate you. Oh, yes, and excuse*

*me for having an affair with your wife, just to top things off. And
for you losing all your money, your reputation, your job, your house,
your car, your—* Ray stopped just on the verge of screaming. It
wasn't what he'd come for. He took a deep breath.

"There was a time I hated you and your dad. But I was at
fault, too. I'm trying to put my life back together, and if I dwell
on the past it's just going to eat me up. I accept your apology.
Now let's move on." He was screaming inside, but he knew it
was how he had to handle it or he'd go insane.

Robbie nodded. He seemed to sense he shouldn't say more.
A menacing tension hung in the air. "Thank you, Ray. Tell
me—how I can help you and your son?"

Ray took another deep breath and laid out the case against
Underwood. He discussed the danger Tommy was in and their
plan to shift the attention away from him. He went into detail about what they knew and didn't know about Underwood,
including speculation about the phony captain, the strange encounter in the parking lot at Sears, and the attack at Risso's. He
said they planned to follow a strategy of focusing on the chief's
incompetence rather than trying to expose his corruption, at
least until they had solid evidence.

Robbie nodded. "I've been thinking about the chief for a
while now," he said. "A few months ago, I asked one of our
investigative reporters to look into the police department. He
spent months digging and talking to people. We didn't have
enough to accuse the chief of anything, but what we saw was
a pattern of unusual decisions by him. He was often involved
directly, personally, in decisions about what cases to pursue and
who to charge. It didn't smell right to our guy. He also said
word on the street is that the vice division has become nothing

more than a gang of cops. So, Ray, I'm one hundred percent behind trying to weed this guy out. I'll write an editorial for Sunday's paper and, if you and Tommy agree, I'd like to make a reference to the police department threatening reporters. If one reporter is threatened by the police, that's a threat to all of us."

"That sounds good. Best not to mention Tommy specifically, but a general editorial about the importance of a free press and how an overly secretive police department infringes on that would start things off right."

"By the way, Ray, I sure don't want to step on Bill's toes, but if Tommy ever needs a job, tell him to come see me. I admit, I read his column—wouldn't miss it for the world. He has real talent."

"Speaking of Bill, he'd like to meet with you sometime. I'm sure you'd have a lot to talk about."

"Well, there's another surprise. I'll give him a call. I think we should talk."

The meeting over, Ray left. Everything had gone well. He breathed a sigh of relief.

"All rise. This court is now in session, the Honorable Judge Kelly presiding."

The judge began. "Be seated. This is an emergency hearing for a victim protective order being sought by Mister Tommy Jacks against Chief Walter Underwood and the Oklahoma City Police Department. Representing Mister Jacks is Joe Louongo." The judge looked up at Louongo and smiled. "Mister Louongo, are you really seeking a restraining order against the chief of police and the whole police department?"

"Yes, your honor. Oklahoma law allows persons who believe they are being harassed and in danger to seek court protection. My client is a reporter for the *OK Journal* newspaper and has been critical of the chief, and as a result we believe the chief has targeted him for harassment by police officers under his control."

The judge made a face. It was obvious he didn't like the whole thing. He noticed a contingent of reporters from print and television filling the pew-like benches. He returned his attention to Louongo and seemed to stare, possibly trying to decide what to say. "The normal purpose of this type of hearing is for the court to grant an emergency restraining order without any notification to the party being named in the restraint, so that party is unaware of the order until served by sheriff deputies. But Mister Louongo, there appears to be an unusual number of members of the press present for this hearing. May I ask why you requested an emergency hearing without notification to the chief, but apparently notified the press?"

"Your honor, we believe that my client's life is at immediate risk. This is unusually important, and requires immediate action precisely because it *is* the chief of police, who has armed police officers whom he can direct to carry out actions against my client without anyone being aware that it isn't due to my client committing a crime, but rather arises from a personal agenda. We have no recourse but to seek court protection so that a tragedy doesn't occur right before our eyes. Time is of the essence to stop a murder."

The people in the front rows could clearly see the judge roll his eyes. "This is utterly without precedent. I will not issue an order to direct a legally appointed law enforcement official not to do his job. For all I know, he suspects Mister Jacks of committing a crime and, if I follow your logic, every crook in town should be in here seeking relief from being harassed by the cops."

"I'm sorry, your honor, but I take offense at that remark. There's no reason for you to imply that my client has committed a crime. We came to you as directed by state law to seek relief from dangerous threats, which is our legal right, but because those threats come from the chief of police, you've now questioned *our* integrity."

The reporters in the court room were smiling. The judge was not. "Mister Louongo, you are on the verge of contempt, and I am sure you do not want to go there. I will take this matter under advisement, and we will reconvene tomorrow at two. Court's adjourned." The judge left quickly and did not look happy.

Louongo smiled at Tommy. "Mission accomplished!"

Once again Tommy was going to be part of the story. He knew it made strategic sense, but he wasn't comfortable with it. There were already reports on the radio about the hearing saying the chief was accused in court of threatening to kill a newspaper reporter. And then they named him: Tommy Jacks. The guy at 7-Eleven would be impressed. Tommy hated it.

He headed up to the press room. He knew he needed to write, but his mind was going too fast to sort it out, and he ended up just sitting and staring. Other reporters wandered in, but nobody said anything to him. He kept his back to them and made a list of things to do.

"Hey, Tommy."

Tommy turned around, and there was Chuck, the police beat reporter. "Chuck. Lose your way to police headquarters?"

"Nah, kind of lookin' for you. There were others in here, so I just waited a bit until they left. Can I talk to you?"

"Sure, what's up?"

"I was at that hearing today. That was a pretty ballsy thing to do. I really admire how you stick up for yourself." Chuck looked nervous, and that started to make Tommy nervous.

"What's goin' on?"

"I know lots of things, Tommy. Lots of things. Those cops—I don't think they even see me anymore, like I'm invisible. Plus, in some odd way I think they believe I'm one of them. But I'm not. You're on target about the chief. He's dirty. I can't give you proof, but I know he's helped all kinds of crooks get off and covered up a lot of things. That's why I wanted to see you—to let you know he really is who you think he is, and that means he's really dangerous. I haven't said anything to Fred because I was scared. I can't do what you're doing."

There was a sadness to Chuck that Tommy hadn't noticed before. "Look, Chuck—I'm scared, too. The stuff you did on that Tinker murder—that took guts. Going out every night and dealing with the lowlifes and the cops, that takes guts. You've got a hard job that doesn't get much glory, but you're admired." Chuck smiled.

"There's something I want to pass along to you. I've known about the suspicions on this for some time, but it was just yesterday that I got proof. I decided not to give it to Fred. He's just way too cautious lately, and I think he'd just sit on it." Chuck reached into his jacket and handed Tommy a coroner's autopsy report. "Janet Knight did not die of a drug overdose. She was murdered."

OK Journal

My View—Tommy Jacks

As you may have read or heard or seen elsewhere, there was a hearing before a District Court judge yesterday concerning a petition for a restraining order against the Oklahoma City Police Department and Chief of Police Walter Underwood. The order, if granted by Judge J.D. Kelly, would penalize the police, of all people, if they came any closer than a certain distance to—well, me. Think about that a minute. Usually the police are the ones to enforce a restraining order, which is generally meant to keep someone else away—say, a disgruntled ex-wife bent on evening the score with her louse of an ex-husband.

I've never been married, so my luck's holding out so far on that account. But I have been drawn into three confrontations that resulted in high anxiety and close calls. In two of them, police were involved—not as the cavalry, but as the bad guys. Just so you understand, I don't bring this up out of a desire for attention. Rather, it's because I'm getting attention I could do without. That's why my attorney is asking for the restraining order.

Chief Underwood seems to think his job is to go after me. Even District Judge Kelly told my lawyer, "For all I know, (Chief Underwood) suspects Mister Jacks (that's me) of committing a crime."

If that's the case, your honor, then why have I been threatened, but never told what I allegedly did wrong? I hired a lawyer, but only because I believed I was in danger. If I've committed a crime, it might be nice to know exactly what it was.

The picture isn't entirely clear, but it looks like the Oklahoma City Police Department is a well-oiled, efficient machine that does everything except what it's supposed to do: investigate crimes and catch criminals. The responsibility for that failure—and it is a failure—goes to the top.

Tony Walters of the *Sun* was shot to death last year, but it wasn't Chief Underwood or Oklahoma City's finest who found out weeks later who killed him. Allen Clark of television station KVY was labeled a suicide six years ago, but it wasn't the police who discovered he wasn't. And two former members of the *Sun's* security detail, the wife of a U.S. senator, and a professional baseball player have all died under unexplained circumstances, and the police don't seem interested in protecting the public by finding out whether anyone is responsible and whether justice might be done.

At least the journalists of the city are doing their job. Just about everyone who was available attended the hearing. I promise I don't know who tipped them off. But they have an interest in this, too. They've all heard the stories about how journalists are treated in police states, with endless harassment, threats, and worse from police, the military, and some dictator's goons.

Is that the kind of department Chief Underwood wants to be known for running? ❦

The Sunday Oklahoma Sun

Editorial

It has come to our attention that the administration and leadership of the Oklahoma City Police Department is not in control of law enforcement or its officers.

The facts are clear. The most notable accomplishment of the department lately has been to compel a reporter for another newspaper to seek a restraining order against Chief Walter Underwood and the police under his command. And investigations into the deaths of Janet Knight, wife of our veteran U.S. Sen. Bruce Knight, and Ray Boone, a star third baseman for our 89ers baseball team, seem not to be priorities for Underwood or his staff.

Perhaps the chief should be reminded that he serves at the pleasure of the people of this city, to which there is a limit. For our part, that limit was passed when bumbling incompetence and disregard for public welfare became the prominent characteristics of the police department.

Be assured, Chief Underwood, that every news organization in this city and state will take notice and respond any time you or your officers dare to intimidate an honest reporter who is merely trying to inform the people.

And we suggest most gravely that your department turn its attention to the matters for which you are given responsibility, namely the investigation of real, rather than imagined, crime. All the people of Oklahoma City remember that your job is to protect them. We advise you to remember it, too.

It would be a mistake to take a whole city's attention and disapproval too lightly, chief.

—Robert Gilmore, Publisher

16
LEGAL OR NOT LEGAL

Tommy stopped at 7-Eleven for the morning paper and coffee before heading downtown. The cashier who always seemed to be there gave him a thumbs-up.

"Great job. Bustin' those damn cops over the head is just what we need around here. They hassle everybody."

Tommy read Vince's front-page story about the hearing. It was strange how much he hated seeing his name in the paper when that was what he did—write for a paper, with his name at the top each time. He felt personally exposed. It was not something he wanted.

As usual, Vince was good, even at capturing the judge's tone toward Louongo without saying it had been obvious he thought the applicant's counsel was an idiot. Tommy smiled thinking about the looks on Louongo's face—the guy was a born showman. He realized he should have bought the *Sun* as well, to see how they covered it, but didn't want to go back into the convenience store now. He headed to Larry Alexander's office for his appointment.

"Good morning, Mister Jacks." Patsy gave him a broad smile with a twinkle in her eye.

"Good morning, Miss White." Tommy wanted to grab her and twirl her around in his arms, but he figured her uncle might not like it.

And Larry walked in. "Oh, good, you're here. Come on back." Tommy took a seat at the table in the small conference room, where Larry introduced a silent stenographer.

"Let's get started." Larry projected a no-nonsense approach. It could hardly be in more stark contrast to Louongo's. "First I want you to describe your encounter with Mitch Douglas that day in his office at the capitol. I might jump in for clarification, but for the most part I just want you to recall, as best you can, the details of the incident."

Tommy related the day at the capitol when he and Vince Young went to Douglas's office to ask why a hearing had been postponed, which wound up with Tommy being thrown against a wall and Douglas wrestling a gun away from a Capitol officer.

Larry nodded. "What happened after this incident? What did the police do?"

"I went to the capitol clinic to get checked out; everything was fine. Eventually the police talked to Vince and me, but they mostly were concerned about what we'd write. They told us Douglas was on medication because of his workload, and he had a bad reaction. Then we left."

"Did they say anything about Douglas possibly facing charges because he attacked you?"

"No."

"Was the Oklahoma City Police Department called about this attack?"

"No."

"You said you went to the clinic. Why did you go to the clinic?"

"When he shoved me into the wall, it knocked the wind out

of me. So, while he and the cops were fighting, I could hardly breathe. It probably looked like I'd been hurt. But I wasn't really; just a little stunned."

"Did you write anything about it that was published in the *Journal?*"

"Yes, I wrote about it in my column."

"Did Vince Young write about it in the paper?"

"Yes."

"Explain the difference between your column and Vince's article."

"A column isn't a news story. Vince's article was. He stated facts and quoted people. My column's an opinion piece, which means I'm giving my observations about it."

"So, in your column, did you state things that were not facts?"

"That's not exactly what I meant. I might say a certain bill looks like a boondoggle. That's not a verifiable fact; it's just my opinion. But it's not a lie. I can imply a senator may be nuts, but if Vince wants to actually state something factually about the senator's mental health in a news story, he'd have to get a quote from an authority saying the senator's nuts."

The back-and-forth went on until Larry said he had enough for the time being. Tommy was exhausted. Larry summed up. "As we've discussed, there is very little basis for Douglas's lawsuit. In fact, at this point you appear to be the only one who could sue successfully. So, I think we can safely stick with our strategy of just letting this play out with the *Journal's* attorneys handling the matter. I'll stay in touch with them, and if they want us to, we'll get involved. But your risk in this matter is very small."

"How about pizza for dinner?" Tommy stood before Patsy's tidy desk, smiling.

"I think that's a great idea." She walked Tommy to the door. "I believe the last time we were at Risso's you were almost killed. Maybe we should just take one car so I can protect you." She gave him a wink.

"Sounds good to me. I'm happy to pick you up. But be fore-warned that while my car is no doubt a classic, it's a little past its prime."

"How 'bout if I pick you up?"

"Okay, but you should again be forewarned my apartment is just a bit untidy."

"I'm starting to see a trend here. But I'm pretty sure I can handle it. Give me your address and I'll see you at seven."

Tommy couldn't stop grinning. He gave her his address and said it was okay if she wanted to spark up a bit. She slugged him on the shoulder.

Tommy wanted to see Albright but didn't know whether to try his apartment uninvited. He'd never been there although he had the address. And Albright seemed to go to lengths to see people at Denny's or other neutral corners.

Tommy wanted to talk to him about Janet Knight and the autopsy report that seemed to indicate she hadn't died of an overdose but rather from some kind of poisoning. The report didn't say how that poisoning happened. Did Senator Knight know, or did the police withhold facts from him? And if they did, why?

Then there was the most sinister thought of all. What if

somebody was using Chuck to set a trap for Tommy and the *Journal?* Did it make sense that someone would give Chuck explosive secrets to topple the chief or even a senator? And if they would, then once again, why? What if it was all a plot?

All those thoughts raced through his head outside Larry Alexander's law office. He decided not to try to chase Albright down. It was only about an hour until he would head to the courthouse for the reconvened hearing. Maybe Albright would be there.

He remembered a small deli on Center Street not far from the courthouse. He grabbed a discarded *Sun* from a pile of used papers at the door, found a seat at the counter, and ordered a ham and cheese on rye.

The *Sun's* story on the hearing the day before was much along the same lines as Vince's, with one odd exception. It included a quote from the *Sun's* political reporter, Mike Sanders, who said, "I've only been a reporter in this town for a while, but I have never been hassled in any way by the police. I have, though, had some trouble with Jacks." Tommy almost fell off his stool. They were quoting their own reporter in a news article making veiled accusations against him. Unbelievable! He needed to talk to his dad about Robbie Gilmore, who was supposed to be helping them.

There were fewer reporters in the courtroom that day, but still a decent contingent. He got a wave from Vince.

"We've received notice Louongo will have a news conference on the front steps right after. You going to say anything?"

"No. This is his world. I wouldn't dare steal any thunder from him."

"Did you read the story in the *Sun?*"

"Yeah, I did. What the hell's going on with them? I'm surprised that got past an editor."

"I know. Odd. You need to make a few more enemies." Vince grinned, but his tone was serious.

"I think a lot of this goes back to Steve Marsh. He got his butt kicked by a smaller, and let's say less masculine guy, and somehow blames me. That tubby asshole Mike Sanders hates me because Marsh hates me. Well, at first, he did. After I knocked the wind out of him, he hates me for his own reasons. You know, I'm really a nice guy."

"Yeah, right. And here we are today to see if you can get a restraining order from the cops, the competing paper, other reporters, and politicians. What do you have to say, slugger?"

"Not funny." But it was.

Louongo was wound up and ready to go. "Tommy, you ready? Forgot to tell you, but I'm going to hold a news conference outside right after the hearing. Also, don't worry about what this guy says. He has to put on his show, too. We're getting the publicity we need. I think you're bulletproof already."

"All rise."

The judge walked in and waved that everyone could sit again. There were established protocols for courtroom decorum, but Judge Kelly was in no mood. "Mister Louongo, I have reviewed your client's request, and it is denied. Since you are an attorney and your client isn't, I'm surprised you allowed this request to proceed. There is no basis in law for a restraining order applied against the police department. It is my opinion you have used this court as nothing more than an attempt to gain publicity. I find this to be a serious violation of your legal ethics, along with an abuse of the court process, and will refer this matter to the state bar for their review. Court is adjourned." Just like the day before, the judge left the courtroom while giving Louongo the evil eye.

Louongo was jubilant. "This is great, Tommy. We're getting what we want. And don't worry about me, it won't hurt me any. The state bar has no balls; they won't do anything. And I'll get a bunch of new clients because of the publicity and the fact the judge hates me—all my potential clients hate judges." He gave a thumbs-up and headed to the front steps, where he proclaimed, "For all you who were inside, you just witnessed one of the problems in our state. The courts and law enforcement are on the same team, and the rest of us on another. The judge denied our perfectly reasonable request for court protection from an out-of-control police department, led by its chief. This is the sort of protective order given many times every day to other citizens when one of their fellow citizens is a danger to them. But because Tommy Jacks's threat comes from the police department, the judge says it's not his problem—just go away. Thanks for nothing, Judge Kelly. But if something happens to Tommy Jacks, let it be on your head. Thank you." Louongo paused for effect, then looked up at the crowd. "I am too upset for questions. Good day."

Tommy drove home, smiling mostly because of his date with Patsy, of course, but also because of Louongo. The man had a gift for driving people nuts. He couldn't imagine what the judge would do if he saw Louongo's so-called news conference on TV. He laughed out loud.

Besides his date, he also had a deadline to meet. He preferred to do his writing in the press room. Due to his schedule being so erratic lately, he'd secured an old typewriter from the *Journal* and arranged a makeshift desk at home. He was getting pretty good at putting his thoughts on paper quickly. When he'd done projects at school, he would write and rewrite, and rewrite again. Now he did the best he could and moved on. He called in his copy just ahead of deadline.

Tommy got ready for his date a bit early and sat down to wait on the small porch. No reason to subject Patsy to the inside of his comfortable, but untidy, apartment. Right on time, she pulled up. She got out holding something, but his eyes were only on her.

"You definitely know all about sparking up." Tommy realized he was falling for Miss Patsy White. "You look great. What's in the bag?"

"Beer. I've got Chinese food in the car. How 'bout we just stay here tonight?"

"That would be fantastic. I did tell you how wonderful you are, didn't I?"

"Not yet you haven't. But we have time."

OK Journal

My View—Tommy Jacks

One quick item before moving into more comfortable news: District Judge J.D. Kelly, as you may have heard, denied this reporter's petition for a restraining order against the Oklahoma City Police Department as operated under Chief Walter Underwood.

This would have been all right if the honored judge had not given for sole justification his contention that this reporter's counsel "used this court as nothing more than an attempt to gain publicity," which the judge deemed "to be a serious violation of . . . legal ethics," among other complaints about my counsel he saw fit to mention. And all of it might be so, but there's still a problem: the attorney isn't the one who needs the restraining order. That would be me. But I guess somebody forgot me. It seems if the judge doesn't like a lawyer, then said lawyer's client is just plain out of luck, no matter what the problem is.

And yes, it's kind of risky to criticize a sitting judge in print, even on the editorial page, which is where we find ourselves. But there seems to be a pattern here, and as averse as I might be to giving my attorney, one Joe Louongo, too much credit, he did identify that pattern in front of a crowd of reporters on the courthouse steps. "The courts and law enforcement are on the same team," as he put it, "and the rest of us are on another."

That "rest of us" includes you, if you aren't a cop or a judge. And that's too bad, isn't it? ✿

17
REPORTER'S REPORT

All Tommy wanted was to sleep in and dream about his night with Patsy. He rolled over and put his hand where Patsy had been. He still felt under her spell and nothing could break the wonderful feeling. All he could do was smile. With regret, the real world interrupted his contented thoughts. He had to get up. The dreaded interview with Senator Knight had to be dealt with. He still wasn't ready for it, but he was tired of worrying about it. He had to get it over with.

He'd canceled all sorts of things lately—meetings with June or Fred and even Vince. He'd canceled dinner with Tracy and his dad. If he could have gotten hold of Albright, he would have set up and canceled a meeting with him. He felt out of control, running from one crisis to the next. He wanted order. He liked schedules, punctuality, and organization, even if his living space was opposed to it.

No one had told him what to wear, but he felt sure his usual blue jeans and jacket weren't appropriate to meet with a U.S. senator. Managing to find a suit that wasn't trashed was no easy task. Once dressed, he felt uncomfortable—one more thing to dislike.

The senator's office was downtown in a storefront that looked like an old campaign office. He got the feeling Knight didn't spend a lot of time there.

He was greeted by a middle-aged woman who remained seated. "How can I help you, sir?"

"My name's Tommy Jacks. I'm here to meet with Senator Knight." Tommy smiled. There didn't appear to be anyone else in the front part of the office. He counted eight clearly vacant desks.

"Is the senator expecting you, Mister Jacks?" Her words and movements were slow and deliberate. "Yes." Tommy waited while she absorbed the new information.

"It's okay, Mrs. Wilson," the senator said, coming out of an office behind her desk. "I was expecting Mister Jacks. We're going into my office now. Could you just take messages on any calls for a while? We'll probably be about an hour." He looked up at Tommy. "Please come in."

The senator led him to a small coffee table between four folding chairs. "This office doesn't handle much anymore. A couple of years ago, we moved it all out to Warr Acres. But Mrs. Wilson's been with me for more years than I can remember. She lives just a few blocks from here and would have had trouble traveling to the Warr Acres office, so I kept this office open mostly for her. When I'm in town I like to spend time here just to visit with her."

That didn't fit into Tommy's image of the all-powerful senator. Could he make something like that up? "She seems very nice."

"Well, Tommy—okay if I call you Tommy?"

"Sure, Senator." Tommy wanted to ask if it was okay to call him Bruce, but he'd promised himself he wouldn't say anything stupid.

"I've read some of your columns. I was pleased when I learned you'd be writing this piece. You're a very talented young man."

"Thank you, sir. I'm still learning, but I have a lot of help." Tommy paused just a little. "Let's get started. I'm very sorry about your wife. Have you been able to finalize arrangements for her services?"

The senator eyed Tommy in a way that suggested he thought that odd for an opening question. "No. There have been some delays in the coroner's report. I've talked to Chief Underwood, and he's assured me her remains will be released within a day or two. Once that happens, all arrangements will be made and announced. My wife was a vital part of my life for a long time, and this is a very difficult period for me." The emotion in his voice seemed real.

Tommy rationalized it would have been weird of him not to ask. "I guess there were some questions at first about the cause of death. Do you know if there's an official conclusion as to that?" He could see by the reaction that he'd entered a subject Knight hadn't expected and didn't appreciate.

"Yes, well, not an official determination. Apparently she died of a heart attack, but they're being very careful to look at all areas. Still, there's no question she died of natural causes after a long illness. Tommy, I know you feel this is part of why I'm in town, and of course I can understand that as a reporter you need to ask, but I think that's all I have for you on the matter."

The hint to butt out couldn't have been clearer. Tommy nodded and moved on. "You're a Democrat, and part of the Democratic leadership team in the Senate. But you were a vocal supporter of President Nixon in the last election. Why would a Democrat support a presidential candidate from the other party?"

The irate look from the senator told Tommy he was doing a good job. "As most Oklahomans know, party labels can be misleading. I'm a conservative Democrat, and President Nixon represents many of my beliefs about how a national government should be run. I'm a lifelong Democrat, and my leadership and tenure-based committee positions in the Senate bring many benefits to the people in Oklahoma. And I might add, while the registration in Oklahoma is still a Democrat majority, Nixon won the state. Hubert Humphrey is no doubt a fine man, but his political beliefs do not align with mine or those of the majority of Oklahomans."

"Do you support the war in Vietnam?"

The senator looked up quickly. Tommy estimated he might just manage to get in one more question before the senator had Mrs. Wilson toss him out. "I believe in freedom. If you're not willing to defend freedom, and I mean with the ultimate sacrifice, you will eventually lose it. We are a God-fearing, Christian country, and we cannot have communists taking over critical parts of the world. I think the young men who are fighting for all of our rights are the best people in this country, and we need to honor them every day."

Tommy turned to a couple of legislative matters that had impact on Oklahoma farmers. He could see Knight relax more while talking about his fine work in Washington supporting the lifeblood of Oklahoma: the family farm. The senator expanded on this area and discussed new programs he was supporting that would help both farmers and ranchers. He also praised the PTA, FHA, and the Boy Scouts.

"One last question, Senator. We discussed Vietnam a little earlier. What do you think about the street protests and the protests against the war at colleges?"

"I think it is a damned shame that so many of these young people are being misled by the press and TV reports about this war. I believe we are doing the right thing to defend our country, and I believe the majority of Oklahomans agree with me."

"Thank you, senator." Tommy wanted to run away before the senator, annoyed all over again, decided to hit him.

"Tommy, you're a tough reporter." The senator chuckled, relaxing a bit. "Had me going on some of those questions, but you did a good job. We need people like you. I imagine our politics are different, and of course I almost never agreed with your dad, but that was a good, hard-hitting interview. Thanks for making me defend what I believe in. Good job." The senator extended his hand and looked Tommy in the eye.

Back in his car, Tommy let out a breath, relieved it was over. But he had a new impression of the senator, and it was confusing. He didn't agree with Knight on much, but there was an odd decency to the man that didn't fit neatly into what he'd been told. Maybe all politicians had a chameleon-like ability to change to fit any situation.

Tommy wanted to talk to Albright. As he drove out of downtown, he spotted a pay phone. He had two numbers to contact him with but didn't think the man ever answered either of them. He dug around and found a dime in the back seat.

"Yeah, what do you want?" Albright growled the words into the phone as if he knew who was calling.

"It's Tommy. Can we meet?"

"Where are you?"

"On Reno, just leaving downtown."

"Meet me at Triple's in about thirty minutes." He hung up.

Tommy thought maybe Albright's constant rudeness was typical of New Yorkers. But if that was so, how did people there keep from killing each other?

Triple's wasn't doing a lot of business. It was after their lunch rush, and too soon for the early drinkers. Tommy settled in near the front door and ordered a beer, mostly as booth rental. Albright appeared, looking winded. "What, are you becoming your dad? Sitting in a bar in the middle of the day, drinking?"

Tommy wondered, not for the first time, how someone like Albright could have become such an integral part of his life. "Good afternoon to you, too, Mister Albright."

Albright frowned, then signaled the waiter to bring the same. "Been reading your stuff. You're getting better."

My God, that was almost a compliment. "Thanks. I try." Tommy took a sip. "Had my interview with Knight this morning."

"How'd it go?"

"I think I made him mad a couple of times. But it surprised me how well he handled it. I don't agree with him on much, but he defended his positions more reasonably than I expected."

"I never paid too much attention to him until I ended up in this town. Seems like he's doing okay in Washington. But he's not very much connected to the state he represents." Albright's beer arrived. He took a sip and seemed to relax.

"I'm not real sure what he believes. I get this feeling with a lot of politicians. It's like they're playing roles. As long as they stay in character, everything's fine and predictable. But if they drop the façade, there's a different person back there."

Albright shook his head. "I've never had much respect for politicians—it's their ability to lie so goddamn easily. When I managed Bill's campaign, I got a different perspective. His opponent lied about almost everything. He'd actually contradict a lie he'd tell one week with a new and different lie the next. Most were easily disproven, if anyone cared to check. So I saw the problem wasn't so much the politicians as it was the people. They believed lies that fit what they wanted to believe. This country isn't going to shit because of politicians. It's because of the rubes who believe them."

Albright's perspective on almost everything was cynical. Still, Tommy tended to agree with him. "The reason I wanted to talk to you is about Knight, but not the interview. Chuck, the police beat guy at the *Journal,* gave me a copy of this autopsy report on Janet Knight." He handed it to Albright. "If I'm reading it right, it says she didn't die of natural causes, but she was poisoned. Murdered."

"Chuck? Who in hell would give him something that explosive?"

"Someone in the coroner's office, maybe, if they wanted to expose the chief doing a cover-up. I'm not sure about any of it. I have no reason to doubt Chuck, but I haven't shown this to anyone. And I sure as hell didn't bring it up with Knight. I did ask him why an autopsy report hadn't been issued, though. He said there'd been a delay but there was no doubt she'd died of natural causes. He also made it clear I should butt out."

Albright examined the report. "Considering everything else that's gone on, I think you have to assume this is a forgery. And I think you have to consider the notion that Chuck is somehow involved with the chief in an attempt to bring you down. The chief is fighting for his very existence, and that makes him a very dangerous man."

18
LEGALLY INSANE
OR JUST CONFUSED

The legislative session was in its final days. Tommy felt like he'd missed a lot of the behind-the-scenes stories since he had not been around as much. His time in the comfortable, usually vacant press room had been reduced by his legal problems and the new habit of writing at home. If you're not visible, people don't feed you gossip.

He made the rounds, dropping into Bud Evans's office to learn a tidbit or two and chat with his friend Gail. He also visited the governor's office. He had no connections to Butler's camp but needed to make himself more noticeable if he wanted to develop any. The governor had the largest staff in the building, and Tommy knew some of them. He casually dropped Senator Knight's name, although he felt embarrassed about it. He got an odd comment from one of the key aides about the governor being upset with Chief Underwood, but no details. Interesting. Later, he tried T.D. McFadden's cubbyhole thinking his dad might be there, but the door was locked.

Back in the press room he worked a little, mostly daydreaming about Patsy until a knock rattled the door. Tommy jumped. Usually nobody knocked—they just walked in. "Come in."

"Oh, hi, Tommy." It was Bart. "I was looking for you. I didn't know if I could just come in or not since I'm not part of the press."

"Sure. Good to see ya. What's goin' on?"

"Hadn't seen you in a while. You okay?"

"Yeah, lots of stuff happenin'. Some good, some bad, but I'm okay."

"Good. Hey, I heard a couple days ago that Mitch Douglas wasn't going to be using his office anymore. They're remodeling it for somebody who's moving up from one of the tiny offices. Thought maybe you might know what happened to your good buddy."

"Huh. No, I haven't heard. Guess it could be almost anything. But kicking him out of his prime office space sounds pretty daring for the weak-kneed party leadership. The old Douglas would be down here raising hell. Have you seen him lately?"

"Nope. I don't think he's been here for days. I was at one of the hearings where he's chairman, and he wasn't there. Nobody said anything."

Tommy wondered what that might mean and how it might impact the lawsuit Douglas had against the paper and him. He got some more inside items about the capitol until Bart said he had to get back to work.

Tommy called June and gave her the gossip news about Douglas. She said she'd make some calls to see what she could find out. She asked him about his interview.

"I think it went okay. I've got some good quotes on the latest farm bill, and a couple of items on Vietnam and the protests. I'll start on it today. When do you want it?"

"We don't have it scheduled, but keep me posted on it. Keep in mind, if you think this has any real news value, we'll want to run it Sunday. So, get me a draft in a day or two, and then we can pin it down."

Just as he was thinking about calling Patsy to see if she was free that night, in walked his newest enemy, Mike Sanders.

"Hello, Tommy. Mind if I use one of the desks?"

What the hell was this? The real Mike Sanders or some imposter? "The room's for everyone in the press. Do what you want." Sanders acted nice and Tommy was surly—what was wrong with that picture?

"Look, I guess I was out of line with you. I shouldn't have said what they put in the paper, so I want to apologize, okay?"

Tommy looked at the pudgy reporter and smiled. "Mike, you're full of shit. Now tell me why you're apologizing to me, or I'll bounce you off the wall again."

Sanders snarled. "You really are an asshole. My boss said I better make things right with you or I could be fired. And I need the damn job."

"Well, that makes sense, at least. Apology accepted. And by the way, I have no reason to feud with you. As far as I'm concerned, we can start over." Tommy turned and went to the far desk and started to type. He heard Sanders mumble something but couldn't make it out.

Tommy kept his head down, and after a while, the phone rang. He looked around. Sanders had left. "Press room."

"I'm getting information on Douglas," June said. "Don't have all the details yet—looks like someone's trying to keep this quiet. He was taken into custody, I think yesterday, and placed in the state mental hospital in Norman. I've got two sources and two slightly different versions. Both seem to say he attacked one of his kids' teachers, a woman. By one account, he broke her arm. Another says she's unconscious in a Stillwater hospital. All this over a bad report card. Both say that after the attack, he went home like nothing happened, and when the police went to talk to him, he pulled a gun. At some point he threatened to kill himself, and then, according to one police officer, he went berserk, yelling obscenities and accusing the officers of being satanic demons."

"My god, the man really is crazy."

"Yeah. Talked to one of our lawyers and gave him what I heard. He said it was very relevant to the lawsuit, and if what I described really happened, he thought they might be able to get it thrown out based on Douglas's state of mind. At any rate, it should at least create some challenges for his lawyers. Guess you can't be nuts and sue for slander."

"Well, that's good. Although at some level I feel sorry for the man. I really do think he's crazy."

"I know. Anyway, got to go. Keep me posted on that Knight feature. I need a few days to get it placed."

"I'm workin' on it. At most I'll have it to you in a couple of days, plenty of time for Sunday's edition. Take care." Tommy hung up. He liked June for a lot of reasons, including her dedication to the paper. He worried about her, too. The *Journal* was her entire life, which wasn't healthy. With that thought, he remembered he'd wanted to call Patsy.

Ray Jacks was winding down his day and looking forward to a quiet evening with Tracy. He had a long list of questions for

T.D., but it seemed he wasn't coming back to the office. Ray didn't know what he did when he was gone, but he was gone a lot, and that troubled him. It was hard to get directions on what T.D. wanted done when he wasn't there. It had been almost a week since Ray last saw him.

He got up from his untidy desk to stretch his legs a bit. Ray preferred to be at the capitol, but with the session ending, that no longer made sense.

Loretta Lynch came in and shut the door. That made the room seem even smaller, so Ray sat back down to give her room to sit.

"Sorry to barge in, Ray, but I have to talk to you."

"Sure, what's goin' on?"

"I'm really worried. I've got to tell you; Mister McFadden needs your help. You might be the only one he'll listen to. I've never been involved in anything like this, and it's literally making me ill. Every night when I go home, I just go to bed, I feel so bad." She sank into a folding chair and started to cry, lowering her head into her lap.

Ray was stunned. "Please, Loretta. Tell me what this is about."

"Over the last couple of months, there have been a lot of unusual transactions going through the car lot accounts. I asked Mister McFadden how I should handle them, and he said just to record them as miscellaneous income, and his tax accountant would handle them at the end of the year. That didn't sound right to me, but I didn't want to challenge him on it."

"How much money are we talking about?"

"Close to three hundred thousand. Then, in the last month, about half that money was taken out, paid to a company called

OKC Investments, Inc."

"Well, I don't know, but I'm guessing T.D. is doing something in real estate. With amounts like that, it would make sense. He must have sold some real estate and then maybe put the money into some other investment."

"That would make sense. But it isn't one big deposit. They're small. A whole lot of them. They're coming from David Harris."

"David Harris?"

"Dealin' Dave. We have transactions with his car lots once in a while. But there's no way car deals would amount to this much money over that short a time. Mister Jacks, I'm a very religious person. I trust God to make things right. I've prayed every night for this to be okay. But it's not just the money. Mister McFadden has been different lately. He spends a lot of time out of touch. He's not at the capitol; he's just not available. He never used to do that. He used to be here every day, going over every detail of his businesses. Maybe it's a woman, I don't know. And that much money? How can it possibly be honest?"

"I'll talk to T.D. For right now, you need to let me handle this, okay?"

"I like my job, and my husband and I need the money. I just didn't know what to do."

"It'll be okay. I'm sure there's a very good explanation." Ray smiled at Loretta in a reassuring way as he let her out of the office, but he was worried. What in hell was going on? Three hundred thousand dollars in a few months based on small deposits? If T.D. was doing something stupid, would he be so dumb as to run the money through his business?

He shut his office door and dialed the phone.

"Press room."

"Tommy, I need to talk to you. Can you meet me at Risso's?"

"Sure, dad. When?"

"Now."

They took a back booth and ordered beer.

"Well, look at us. Father and son, having a drink at Risso's." Tommy's tone bore irony and concern.

"I'm not going back to my old ways, and you should be careful, too." Ray smiled, feeling at ease with his son.

Ray told Tommy what he'd learned about T.D., including the connection with Dealin' Dave. He hesitated to involve the police for obvious reasons, but beyond that, he wasn't sure what to do with the information.

Tommy thought a moment. "Yeah, I'm not sure anyone can trust the police right now. And that goes double for anybody named Jacks. You need to talk to Albright."

Ray gave his son a quizzical look.

"Yeah," Tommy went on. "He knows something about Dealin' Dave. He was physically attacked by him and some goons because he ran a piece or two in *The Banner* about him being involved in prostitution. Of course, Albright didn't have proof—just gossip passed to him. But he's been told Dave and his brother are trying to fill the vacuum left when Big Frank Martin disappeared."

"I wonder if Taylor Albright ever has a normal, boring day."

"He does keep things stirred up, even when he doesn't mean to."

"Why in the world would T.D. get involved in a prostitution ring with Dealin' Dave?"

"Eh, money, sex—*both?*"

"Yeah, dumb question."

19

NEWSPAPER, MEGAPHONE, AND OTHER ARMS

"Well, I'll be a sonofabitch—if it isn't Ray Jacks, right here in Denny's," Albright blurted, a little too loudly.

"Good morning, Taylor. Mind if I join you?" Ray was more accustomed to the early hour than he once was, thanks to years of the prison regimen. He slid into the booth without waiting for a reply.

"I've been getting good reports from your son. Glad things are working out for you." There was a real sincerity in Albright's voice.

Ray had to grin at his old friend. "I've been such a lousy father in the past, it doesn't take much to impress my son. But, all in all, life's not bad. And I owe you for that."

"Okay, enough of this nicey-nice B.S. Why are you here?"

Ray covered what he knew or suspected about T.D. including the connection to Dealin' Dave. "Tommy says you had some run-ins with the guy, and I wanted to get your input on how to handle this."

"First off, I believe your suspicions about T.D. are absolutely right. I've got some good information from a couple of people who said there was someone else involved in the Harris brothers' entry into organized crime. I haven't been able to identify who it is, but with what you've told me, I'm guessing it's probably your guy. Politics and crime just seem to go hand in hand."

"Yeah. I know I could just quit and forget about it, but that seems wrong. And going to the cops or the DA might create more problems than it solves. Any thoughts?"

"You still talking to Bill?"

"Not really. I know a lot about the paper and his problems with it, but that all comes through Tommy. You think I should go to Bill?"

"I'm not sure. I don't talk to him much anymore. Kind of strange, but I think I threaten him in a way. I'm kind of the crazy friend you'd just as soon not see, definitely not in public." Albright smiled, but Ray could see the pain.

"I'd worry that might hurt Tommy somehow," Ray said thoughtfully. "He's doing great, and I sure don't want to cause him any problems. He can't write about this, and I don't want him to. I guess I'll just have to contact someone in the justice system—the FBI, the DA? Feels like I'm going behind T.D.'s back without a good reason. But how can I just ignore it?"

"What about Robbie? You got him to help with the chief. He's your old pal from way back. Maybe you should go see him."

Ray thought about that. There seemed to be some logic to the idea. He knew Robbie was keen on fighting crime and corruption. Here was a two-fer: street crime and political corruption. How could he resist? On the other hand, what would he be able to do? He put the question to Albright.

"He's got a staff of reporters, some investigative. He can get people to do some digging. If they come up with facts, he's got the clout of the state's major paper to make it stick. He can force the police into action without putting you or Tommy at risk. Of course, keep in mind—if you're right, then your job's going to disappear along with T.D.'s freedom."

"Yeah, my job, and jobs for a bunch of other good people. It makes me doubly angry at T.D., putting all that at risk for more money or power or whatever's driving him." There was a flash of the old righteous Ray Jacks for a moment.

Albright changed the subject. "Looks like I'm headed back to New York City."

"I'm surprised you've stayed this long. Why're you going back now?"

Albright looked pleased. "I've written a book about the shit-pile that this country's national politics have turned into, and it's been picked up by a publisher in New York. Could be a bestseller, according to them, so I might as well bask in all that glory in my hometown."

"How 'bout that. Congratulations!"

"Well, still have to get through the editing stage, and I'll probably kill anyone who changes a word." His words seemed angry, but he was smiling.

"A celebrity author in New York City on TV talking about political nonsense foisted upon us lesser humans. How could you want anything else?" Ray was genuinely happy for the man.

"Well, you may find this hard to believe, but I'll miss this place. And don't tell him this, but I'll especially miss your son."

If it wouldn't have been awkward, Ray would have hugged him. "Well, you never know about Tommy. His sights are set pretty high. Maybe in a few years he'll join you in the big city."

Albright chuckled. "Yeah, who knows? Tommy could be a star there. He's good."

They said their goodbyes before they both started crying and started some kind of old-man spectacle.

Waking up late, alone in bed, was an immediate reminder for Tommy to call Patsy that morning. He'd tried the day before but hadn't been able to reach her. He'd brought his unfinished Knight article home to wrap up. First, though, came coffee and checking the mail.

He noticed several envelopes that seemed addressed by the same hand. He opened one. Inside were several documents appearing to be internal memos on Oklahoma City Police Department stationery. And there was a photo of the police chief with a large man Tommy didn't recognize. He read the accompanying memo.

> *To: Tom Lawson, Deputy Chief*
>
> *From: Walter Underwood, Chief of Police*
>
> *Effective immediately the Vice Division will report directly to me. You will no longer have authority over this division. Officers in this division will have authority to take action without approval from elsewhere in the administration, based on my authority. Please advise all department heads about this change in department structure.*
>
> *Also, I want to receive any reports involving Frank Martin or anyone claiming association with Frank Martin. Any arrests or other department action involving these individuals should be referred to the vice division and my office should be immediately notified. This must be kept confidential.*

Tommy read the memo a couple of times. Was there something wrong with this, or did it just sound wrong? Did this mean the department provided protection to Martin, or was Underwood only organizing as a way of keeping tabs on him? He looked at the photo again. Maybe that was Frank Martin, but that didn't prove anything other than the chief knew him. Why would someone send these? He went through the pile of mail, opening four other letters with the same handwriting.

In one was a handwritten list with dates, a number, and a dollar amount. Could be a list of checks, Tommy thought. The thirty or so entries easily totaled about forty thousand dollars. The dates spanned a little less than two months.

Two envelopes contained what appeared to be police department internal documents dropping all charges against certain detainees. There were several names, but no Frank Martin, and all documents were signed by Underwood.

Other documents seemed to be pages out of an address book. Tommy glanced through them and saw names he knew, like Billy Ray Watts, David Harris, and T.D. McFadden. Was this the chief's address book? As he read over the pages again, he saw "Chuck Branson." Chuck from the police beat. What did that mean?

Tommy checked for any indication of who sent them, but found nothing. All were addressed by the same person, with no return address. All were mailed from somewhere in the city.

Did he have something, or would this turn into nothing on closer inspection? He drank his coffee while he re-examined each item. There was nothing really damning in the documents. Directing the vice division to report to the chief could be legitimate—just a routine organizational directive. Even tracking Martin might be something the chief wanted for law enforcement reasons. Signing the release documents might be damaging, but he didn't know the names. Maybe they were Martin's goons and maybe not. Maybe they were random people who'd been wrongly charged in the first place and the chief had made things right. And the address book might contain names of friends or enemies. It didn't mean anything by itself.

If he knew who'd sent them to him, that might be the biggest lead. But there seemed to be no clue who that was. He knew he needed to get back to writing, but he called Patsy first.

"Law office of Lawrence Alexander, may I help you?" said the melodic voice.

"Can I talk you into take-out Chinese tonight?"

"Nope." There was a pause. "But take-out hamburgers and fries from Johnny's would be wonderful. See you about six-thirty, and we can go get them together, okay?"

"More than okay—perfect." Tommy smiled. If he stayed on the phone any longer, he might have started dancing.

Jackie Carter had been out of the hospital only two days and was still in a lot of pain. She'd always thought the chief was a pig of a man with an ego the size of the Empire State Building. She never imagined he'd turn violent. She was strong, and she rose through the ranks of the police department despite being female, a major barrier in most police departments and more so in Oklahoma City. She succeeded because she took no nonsense from anyone and was good at her job. Chief Underwood noticed her work—and her good looks—and moved her into his office as his personal assistant. Jackie knew she was attractive and used her looks for leverage with a lot of men. The chief was just another.

She became his trusted assistant. In a few months, she discovered he was on the take. His big deals were with Frank Martin, who'd recruited the chief somehow before Jackie's time and paid him a lot, regularly. The chief seemed to believe he was in charge of the arrangement, but Jackie knew immediately that Martin controlled things.

Still, to control him, she led Underwood to think he seduced her. She was a little repulsed by him because he was more a showman, con man, and goon than a police chief. Before long he began to trust her with secrets, including about Martin. That gave her the chance to gather a damning cache of documents she kept hidden in her apartment as insurance, just in case things went south.

And they did. The trouble started after Martin left town. Big Frank knew how to keep the chief from doing anything stupid, but once he left, Underwood got involved with a trio of amateurs who took over portions of Martin's old empire. How they'd gotten together, she wasn't sure. She suspected that had something to do with T.D. McFadden but had no way to prove it. The remaining two were the Harris brothers, Dealin' Dave and Little Dave. They were jokes. She could see immediately they didn't know what they were doing and would get everyone strung up by sheer stupidity.

The risks became too great. She confronted Underwood about the morons. Their conversation went downhill after she pointed out that if it hadn't been for Martin's street smarts, the chief would probably already be in jail. Underwood wasn't fast, but he was big, and he had a temper. He began beating her, out of control. She lost consciousness, and when she woke, she knew she was badly hurt. After gathering her strength and her nerve, she crawled to the phone. She told the police who accompanied the ambulance that she'd been attacked in her apartment by a burglar but managed to scare him off before passing out. She gave them a fake description that would match a huge pool of suspects.

Jackie spent two weeks in the hospital. The chief never visited her, and neither did anyone else from the department. After her release, she returned to her apartment to get her hoard of evidence. Then she checked into a downtown hotel, packing a gun and cash. She sent documents that wouldn't give too much away to the *Journal's* columnist, Tommy Jacks, just because he seemed to have it in for Underwood.

The next move was uncertain. First, she had to heal. Then she would decide how to use the gun. The chief hadn't seen the last of her.

20

BIGOTS, BASEBALL, AND SURPRISES

Billy Ray Watts only spent one night in jail before he was bailed out, and he swore he'd never go back. He'd die first. His biggest concern, then, was the fact he was guilty. He'd shot Ray Boone and, given the opportunity, he'd shoot the bastard again. Nobody talked to Billy Ray the way Boone did. He was also charged with resisting arrest and threatening police officers. His attorney, Joe Louongo, was loud and showy, but he tried to be candid with Billy Ray. He told him things looked bad. So Billy Ray fired him and hired a new lawyer who said maybe he could work it out. His new attorney had a reputation even worse than the first big mouth, but he knew how to talk to egomaniacs. David Watts—no relation, or at least not that he'd admit—knew the only way to avoid life in prison for his client would be a plea deal maybe for twenty years, with a bit of luck and the right judge. Of course, if he told Billy Ray that, he'd be fired just like the first guy and never collect his fee. So he kept quiet and listened while the buffoon shouted his head off.

How Billy Ray became owner of the Oklahoma City 89ers was a little foggy even to him. He had a rather serious drinking problem that tended to erase some memories. Still, he seemed pretty sure it had to do with a real estate deal that somehow ended up including the team. Billy Ray was a wealthy white supremacist and con man, which did not prevent his approval as owner of a minor-league team. He also had a massive ego. He quickly decided he knew more about baseball than anyone else, although he knew very little.

During his first year of ownership, he got rid of all of the non-white players. As a result, the 89ers suffered the worst season in minor league baseball history. Realizing he might have miscalculated, he brought back some Latin players, though he told anyone who would listen they were inferior because they couldn't speak English while he, of course, could. Once he'd brought in four very good ones, the team bounced back to a winning record. All that really achieved was to identify Watts as a lousy, bigoted human being. He didn't care.

His players, to a man, hated him. They respected their fellow athletes and admired each other's talents regardless of heritage. The most popular on the team were called the "three amigos" by the local press. They were the heart and soul of the 89ers, even if the owner publicly ridiculed them.

"Bill Nicholson to see you." Billy Ray's secretary announced over the intercom.

"Send him in."

The team's manager didn't beat around the bush.

"Billy Ray, we've got a rebellion on our hands. They all went on strike."

"Strike! Fire everybody, right now!" Billy Ray didn't handle bad news well.

"A little late for that. They're out in front of the stadium with signs—they say some pretty bad things about you." Nicholson was an old baseball man with no interest in anything else, and desperately needing to keep his job.

"Everybody?"

"Yep. Rosen, Lemon—all of 'em. You know, Rosen was a friend of Boone's. He told me if you don't sell the team, you'll regret it."

"That weak-armed pitcher is threatening me? I'll shoot the bastard." Billy Ray got up and began pacing rather close to his display of antique firearms. Nicholson got nervous, and it crossed his mind, not for the first time, that he might join the players out front. Everybody knew Billy Ray was nuts. But to see him in action was unnerving.

"Might be a good idea if you left before things got worse."

Billy Ray gave his manager the evil eye, but after some thought, decided, "Yeah, maybe so." He pushed the intercom button and barked, "Have my driver bring my car around back."

He had been working on a plan the last few days. He'd transferred all his cash to a bank in South Africa, and as a precaution carried his most important documents with him. He'd also discovered that, due to an odd twist of international law, he couldn't be extradited from South Africa since he potentially faced the death penalty. It made him want to go back to the stadium and shoot more players. He headed to the airport instead.

Billy Ray was out on bail, so his ability to travel was restricted. According to the judge's order, he wasn't allowed to leave the state, let alone the country. But communication between the state courts and the United States Immigration and Naturalization Service was nearly non-existent. No one questioned him before he boarded a flight.

He would find much in common with the power elites in South Africa.

Ray had hardly spoken to Robbie Gilmore in forty years, and now he had his second appointment with the man in a week. He wasn't sure how Robbie would react to his news.

Robbie seemed on edge and distracted. "Ray, come in, come in. Have a seat."

"Sorry to bother you. Got a situation in my world, and I thought it might be of interest to you." Ray went on to describe the strange relationship between T.D. McFadden and the Harris brothers. He emphasized he had no real facts, only speculation. He told Robbie what Loretta Lynch said, which also didn't prove anything but seemed awfully suspicious nonetheless.

Robbie frowned. "Funny. I would have guessed T.D. to be better than something like this, assuming he's involved. Why do you think he'd do this?"

"Well, my son guessed it was just money, and maybe sex. But I think this is completely out of character. I think there's something more to it than that."

"Ray, look—I have a few things on my mind today. My father's taken a turn for the worse. I think this is the end."

Ray sighed. "I'm sorry."

"No need. He had a long, successful life. And he'd be the first to tell you he'd rather be dead than only partly alive, hooked up to a machine. I think the man never actually contemplated his death. He never made arrangements, never gave instructions." He sighed again. "One of his doctors called and said it wouldn't be long."

The room was quiet for a moment.

"You should go," Ray said. "We can discuss all this another time."

"It's okay. It could be hours. Or days—who knows? I just wanted to let you know why I'm distracted. I'd rather be here talking to you than sitting in that damn hospital." Robbie smiled weakly.

Ray nodded. He had experience with hospitals and grief. "Yeah. I'm not sure how you'd tackle this thing with T.D. and Dealin' Dave. But I thought you might have someone do a bit of investigating and see what turns up."

"Well, I'm not sure what we'll do, exactly. But we'll do something. This is a big story on several fronts. I'm a little short of good people right now, but this'll be a priority. I'll want to get all the information, even speculation, that you have. And of course, the documents that employee has." Robbie paused, reflecting for a moment. "Would you be interested in going to work for me?"

"Me? Nah, I'm not a reporter. Or an editor."

Robbie shrugged. "I've got people for that. I need someone who can think. It's not a fully developed idea, but I can see you managing a department that does investigative reporting with an emphasis on politics. It'd be staffed with a rotating pool of reporters, but you'd be the permanent head, driving the agenda and tracking down stories. The reporters would write, but you'd keep them focused. I think it would fit you, Ray. What do you think?"

Sonofabitch, is what he thought. Could he really do that? Would he want to do that? "Wow, um—it's a surprise. I'm not sure what I think. You sure we could work together?"

"Hell, yes, we can. We were friends, and then we were ene-mies, though it should never have happened that way. Very few people know each other as well as we do. I trust you, and you should trust me. We've seen our best and, for sure our worst. I think we'd make a great team."

Go to work for the enemy, the man he'd hated for years, the man who'd put him in prison, and the man he'd cursed every day and every night from a miserable cell. How bizarre could life get? But he *could* do that. Ray knew every nook and cranny of the political world, and he was an experienced observer of people. He could manage people, and there was no one more dogged in pursuing a lead, digging out the truth, and stomping on the bad guys. He had a muckraker's heart.

"I like the idea. There might be a problem, though, with my soon-to-be wife, Tracy Clark. I know you know her because of her dad and of course, the tragedy with Judy Jackson. She and I are living together. And other than my son, she's the most important person in my life. She just lost her job at the TV sta-tion, and we've been talking about moving so she can continue her career. I owe her a lot. If she has to move, I will, too."

"Didn't she use to work for KVY?"

"Yeah. She was fired by the guy who replaced her father be-cause she wanted to go on the air after she found out he was dead. Since then she's worked at about every station in town, but they always end up saying they're looking for younger people."

Robbie shook his head. "Man, my life is just full of screw-ups. I didn't know she was fired back then. I would've put a stop to that, because she was great. That moron you're talking about only lasted a few months. I guess I wasn't paying attention to anything except myself back then. But jeez, I can fix that. D'you think she'd be willing to come back to KVY?"

"I don't know. She holds a grudge, so I'm not sure."

"Shit, she *should*. Just wait here. I need to talk to someone." Robbie left. Ray was still thinking about everything that was happening and what it could mean for him and for Tracy when Robbie stormed back in.

"Just talked to the KVY manager. He says Tracy'd be perfect to fill an opening we have for a morning anchor. He said her hard news background and personality is just what he's looking for—someone with instant credibility with the audience. He thinks with her he could win back the time slot—he's all excited, wants to talk to her immediately. Should he call?"

Ray was impressed. "Let me talk to her first."

"You could actually work for Robbie Gilmore after all that's happened? The man probably caused my father's death. Maybe he didn't order it, but his goons sure as hell killed him. It was his lies that put you in prison for years. You can just let that go?" To say that she held a grudge might not quite have covered the depth of Tracy's bitterness toward Robbie Gilmore.

"I don't know, Tracy. I'm not sure what to do. That's why I wanted to talk with you about it. I just told you what happened. I wasn't expecting anything like this. But you need a job, and I need a job, and he seems genuinely remorseful, and he's acknowledged his mistakes. You tell me what we should do." Ray'd had more time to think about it, and he knew the job was something he wanted. But was he willing to make a deal with the devil in order to get it? He didn't know.

"It just makes me sick. I don't have any answers. I'm just furious." Much of her anger, from the look in her eyes, was aimed at Ray—the messenger.

"Okay, I'll just tell him no. We'll move. We can find other jobs, we'll be okay. I'll call and tell him no."

"No. I don't know. Just give me some time. Shit, I hate this."

Ray got up and gave Tracy a hug. "I love you."

Tracy smiled and began to cry. Ray didn't know why, but he didn't need to.

Jonathon H. "J.H." Gilmore was pronounced dead at nine that evening in his private suite at Saint Anthony Hospital. The attending physician noted he died peacefully in his sleep. Hospital records indicated he was ninety-six. No one other than hospital staff were present. A message was left for Robert Gilmore at the *Sun* headquarters, but he didn't return the call.

OK Journal

My View—Tommy Jacks

Hope you're sitting down before you read the next few words.

It's time to sympathize with, and stand up for, the Oklahoma City Police Department—at least for this one thing that happened, or didn't happen.

What didn't happen is this: the state courts and the U.S. and Immigration and Naturalization Service didn't share information, even when a person charged with murder bought a ticket not only to leave the state, but the country, after having been firmly ordered by a judge to do neither.

The upshot is that our Oklahoma City 89ers, mired in a six-game losing streak and beset by disaffection among the players, and having lost their star third baseman to the aforesaid murder, have now also lost their owner.

That last loss might be the best news the team has heard in a while. Ray Boone, according to every player on the roster—from veteran pitcher Al Rosen to up-and-coming outfielder Orlando Alvarez—was prized as a teammate. Billy Ray Watts, the owner who alienated every last player on his own team and just about everyone else besides, was not held in similar esteem, to put it lightly.

And now, having taken illegal advantage of the benefit of doubt while police investigate Boone's death, he sits somewhere in Johannesburg, South Africa, far beyond the reach of our state and national law enforcement.

"Good riddance," Alvarez said over the phone. "The only thing that would make me happier is if the people of South Africa were to rise up and—"

As much as we agree with Alvarez's sentiments, it may be best not to repeat the rest of his sentence in a family newspaper. Let's just say he prefers to be rid of Watts and his ilk so he can concentrate on making it to the major leagues, as many predict he will. Still, he brings up a point worth discussing.

"It's true," Rosen sighed. "If you weren't lily white, Billy Ray didn't like you. He just put up with players who weren't because the big club kind of got onto him about it."

Notice the "kind of" part? Even twenty-two years after Jackie Robinson became the first player of color to take a place on a major-league roster, baseball is still getting used to the idea that it's a real American pastime—as in North, Central, South and Latin.

"We've got baseball diamonds all over the island," said Alvarez, who hails from a hardscrabble suburb of Santo Domingo, capital of the Dominican Republic. "And I've played in Puerto Rico, and in Mexico, and in Panama, too. They're crazy for baseball everywhere in Latin America."

As you'll read on the sports page, the 89ers will continue to operate under officials provided by the American Association until a new owner steps in. Whoever that is should be closely scrutinized to make sure he or she won't repeat Watts's mistakes. Those mistakes may or may not have included murder—we don't know that, yet.

And it isn't the fault of Oklahoma City police that they got left holding the bag. They did their job. But somebody out there booted an easy grounder. 🍎

21
CHANGING TIMES

J.H. Gilmore's passing was the big story of the day. Both papers played front-page headlines and extensive obituaries. The governor and the mayors of Oklahoma City and Tulsa were quoted as extending deepest sympathy to the Gilmores. Business leaders also bemoaned the loss of a great leader. No family members were quoted. Memorial arrangements were made to include a special service at the state capitol. Almost no one said anything negative in public about the man or his long history.

Senator Knight's office released a long statement filled with praise, declaring Gilmore's death as the end of an era. He was proclaimed as equal to the founding fathers of the country. Knight said he personally was deeply saddened by the loss of the great man and leader, acknowledging he had been a major influence on the senator's career.

"Jeez, it's like he was a damned saint. Where in the hell are the quotes from everybody who knows he was an asshole?" Albright marveled.

Tommy gave Albright a look of mock dismay. "He died. You publish nice things. It's a law of nature."

Tommy had dropped off his Knight article at the paper early that morning and then stopped by Denny's to see if Albright was in his usual spot. He was, and he ignored Tommy's sarcasm. "What's your impression of Knight now that you've interviewed him?"

"He's smarter and nicer than I'd expected. Not sure what I think about him. I had him pegged as a pompous womanizer who'd abandoned his wife and had little to do with the people he represented. Now I have a different picture."

"Well, don't lose your edge just because these people seem nice when you meet them. You don't become a U.S. senator without an ability to convince people that you have their best interests at heart. Knight's been at this a long time, so he's a master at saying whatever sounds right in the situation while never saying anything you can turn into a real commitment."

"Yeah. My dad once told me really bad people make great politicians because they lie so easily, and really good people would never be elected because they cannot lie."

"I thought Bill Anderson was someone who could break that mold," Albright sighed, "but I guess the election results showed otherwise."

"I heard a rumor you're on the verge of becoming a bestselling author and leaving the sticks for the big city lights. Any truth to that?"

Albright shrugged. "Some, but only a little. I'm going to have a book published, and my publisher thinks it could be a hit. I'm pretty sure he thinks that about every book he publishes—otherwise, why do it? So, yeah, I have a book coming out. Whether it becomes a bestseller is a huge question mark. But I am heading home. That's been on my mind for some time. The book just gave me a push to actually do it."

"Well, hell, bestseller or not, that's incredible news. My dad said it's about politics. Can't wait to read it."

"I've had a lot of help writing it. I'm not the writer you are, but I think it says some things that need to be said. As soon as I get something that's more or less finished, I'll get you a copy. I'd appreciate your input."

Albright had to be leaving; he'd never be this nice if he weren't.

"What's going to happen with *The Banner?*"

"Unless you want to jump in, I guess next week's issue will be the last. Once it goes out, I'll be leaving. Already had most of my stuff shipped back to New York, so I just have to get on a plane."

"It'd be fun to keep *The Banner* going, but I have a feeling Bill Anderson would have something to say about that."

"Yeah, probably. You ought to come see me in New York. I know this is your home, but New York is the center of the universe. The opportunities there for you would be tremendous."

"I'm not ready to leave just yet. Maybe in the future. I would appreciate a phone number that worked."

It was nice they were parting on such good terms. Still, it was a little uncomfortable without their usual caustic back-and-forth.

Tommy left Denny's feeling down. He was going to miss Albright, but there was more to it than that. There was too much unresolved. He wasn't sure how to deal with his suspicions about Chuck, or the autopsy report he carried around. If it was true, Janet Knight was murdered. He couldn't ignore that. And there was the dead airman at Tinker. The Air Force had said nothing about it, other than it was none of his business. Chuck was connected to that loose end, too. He'd been stationed at Tinker, worked at the base paper, and now he was assigned to look into the death for the *Journal*. Nobody was saying anything about the dead guy, including the press. It was Tommy's job to keep the pot stirring. The more he thought about it, the more everything seemed to lead back to Chuck. He spotted a pay phone.

He called the *Journal* and asked to speak to Chuck Branson. There was a pause, and then the receptionist came back. "Sorry, sir. Mister Branson no longer works here." Tommy hung up. What the hell was that—he no longer worked there? He called the paper back and asked to speak to June.

"Hello."

"I was just told Chuck no longer works for the paper. What's going on?"

"Hey, Tommy. Thanks for getting the Knight feature to me, it looks great. About Chuck, I'm not sure. Fred told me he called and quit. He asked why, but Chuck just said he had his reasons. Do you know anything?"

"No." He hadn't told anyone at the paper about the autopsy report. "I need to get hold of him, though. Do you have his home phone, or maybe an address?"

"I don't think—normally—shit." She sighed. "I'm going to help you, but this is a favor, okay? You can't tell anyone. Just a minute." She put the phone down and Tommy heard her speaking to someone on another phone before she came back. "This is weird. Personnel doesn't have anything on him. Betty down there said when he was hired, he told her he was just getting settled and didn't have a phone or permanent address yet, and when he did, he would get them to her. But he never did.

So, we don't know how to get hold of him."

Shit. "Okay. I'm headed back to the press room. Maybe you could ask around and see if anyone hung out with him after work or something. Maybe they'd know how to get hold of him."

Tommy called the *Journal* again, this time to ask for Vince. "This is Vince."

"Tommy. Can you meet me for a beer at Risso's at about five?"

"Is this a date, Tommy?"

"*Yes, I want to ask you to marry me.* Are all newspaper people wise-asses?"

"You're not my type, and yes, all newspapermen are wise-asses. *You should know.* See you at five."

Tommy got back to the empty press room and spent time on his column. He recalled Albright said he was putting out a last issue of *The Banner*; he sure wanted to get his hands on one. He also thought about calling his dad to see how he and Tracy were doing, but he knew he'd be asked over, and he was already going to meet Vince. If he told his dad that, Ray might wonder if he was making excuses—they still felt awkward around each other. It was odd that, even after coming a long way from being estranged, they still found it hard to just be normal around each other.

The press room phone rang. "Tommy Jacks."

"Tommy, June. Asked around. Looks like our Mister Chuck didn't associate with anyone. A couple of people said he was a loner, and turned them down if they invited him to have a drink or lunch or whatever. One guy said Chuck scared him. I thought he was just weird because of his job, but it looks like he was weird all the time."

Not good. It made Tommy nervous. "Okay. Thanks, June. Workin' on some stuff. I'll call tomorrow and fill you in." He hung up before she could ask what it was.

"I thought about it all day." Tracy looked determined, but worried. "Of course you should take the job with Robbie. And I should take the job with KVY. Tommy's here, and we should stay if there's any way that we can. If it doesn't work out for either one of us, we move."

It was clear a decision had been made, and there would be no discussion. Ray nodded. "Yeah. I'm a lot more worried about my part than yours. You're going to do great, and if we decide a move makes sense later, it'll help you find another anchor job."

They hugged. The decision relieved the tension they'd felt for days. Neither wanted to leave, mostly because of Tommy. But also, neither felt like running away from their pasts for the wrong reasons.

"I'll call the manager at KVY and set up an interview as soon as possible so I don't change my mind." She smiled, a bit slyly. "I guess if you can't locate T.D., all you can do is hand in a resignation letter."

"Yeah, I'm concerned about what is going on with him. But I'm not sure I can help him or his people. I'll call Larry and give him a heads-up. He went out of his way to help me get the job with T.D., and I don't want any misunderstanding about why I'm quitting. He'll be shocked to hear I'm going to work for the evil empire."

"I guess you know you'll have to watch what you say once

you're working for Robbie."

"I know. Gotta work on my attitude. How about we get married?"

Tracy just stared at Ray. Way too long.

"I have no idea why I love you. You have no clue about women, do you?"

"Okay, that was a little abrupt. If the answer's no, I understand. I'm the world's worst husband—I get it. Please don't kick me out." There was genuine fear in Ray's eyes.

Tracy smiled, but she also started to cry. "Yes, I'll marry you." She whispered to Ray.

Senator Knight's office released a press bulletin saying he would not seek reelection in 1972, citing the recent death of his wife and his own declining health, but with no mention of what that meant. It said the senator wanted to make his decision well in advance of the end of his term to allow for an orderly transition. Immediately after the announcement was circulated, responses came from a long list of potential candidates, including Governor Butler.

"It was with tremendous sadness that we hear Senator Knight has decided not to run for re-election. He has served our state and our country with honor. He will be missed by the great deliberative body of the U.S. Senate. With this news, I am considering a run for the Senate. I think that as governor I have demonstrated my understanding of the needs of the people of Oklahoma, and it would be an honor to represent them in Washington, D.C."

Whispers of speculation arose about who the powerful

Oklahoma Sun would endorse now that J.H. Gilmore was no longer in charge. Many had heard long-standing rumors that Robbie Gilmore thought Butler was an idiot. Times were changing.

OK Journal

My View—Tommy Jacks

Respectful silence is understandable in the case of the surprising announcement by U.S. Sen. Bruce Knight, the Democrat who has served so long hardly anyone can recall who had his seat before him (J. Homer Edwards—remember him? Don't feel bad. We don't, either).

The election for Knight's seat won't occur for another three years. That is, unless he decides to follow yesterday's announcement with another saying he's stepping down earlier. Recall from his previous statement that he referred to "declining health," although he offered no details,

and no sources up to now seem to have any idea what he means. A call to the Washington bureau of The Associated Press turned up nothing.

"The Senate's a bona-fide beehive for gossip," said Walter Mears, AP's veteran Washington correspondent. "If he'd been to see a doctor, we'd have had the story before the nurse took his temperature."

Much less a mystery is who controls the Gilmore publishing and broadcast enterprise after the passing of Jonathan H. "J.H." Gilmore. We all know Robbie Gilmore remains at the helm, where he has been since his father's untimely incapacitation last year. But that isn't the whole story. Every capitol expert and veteran in this state of oil, gas, cows and crops has been waiting on the edge of his seat to see how the change in the Gilmore empire will affect political life.

"Make no mistake," intoned Gene Rapier, the Democratic senator from McAlester who was probably the closest thing to a worthy opponent for J.H. Gilmore when things got down to political brass tacks, "the politics of this state are about to change.

And no, I can't say how much."

Meanwhile, even closer to home is the lengthy, uncomfortable silence over the death of Air Force Staff Sgt. Kent Milton at Tinker Air Force Base. We know, because we've been told, that it's military business. But that doesn't mean it's nobody else's business. The man's death still occurred on American soil, in service to Americans. So, it's America's business. That's why someone who takes responsibility seriously should take charge and let people know how and why he died. 🐛

22
TRUST ME, OR NOT

If Tommy had been a drinker, he might have tied one on that night. The feeling in the air was like nothing was right. He sipped his beer and waited for Vince. He reminded himself he would see Patsy later. He smiled. Not everything was going wrong.

Vince showed up, got a Coke, and slid into the booth, raising his tumbler for a toast. "Going to my in-laws' tonight for dinner. Her mother thinks all reporters are drunks. So if she thinks I've been drinkin', I'll have to listen to a thirty-minute sermon on the evils of alcohol. What's goin' on?"

"What do you know about Chuck?"

"Probably less than you. I see him now and then around town. He acts like he doesn't know me—sometimes like he doesn't *want* to know me. Why? What's up?"

Tommy had grown to trust Vince more than anyone else at the paper. They were about the same age, and Vince had always been honest. "Don't know, but one thing's for sure—he just quit under mysterious circumstances." Tommy explained everything that had happened since Chuck gave him the autopsy. He showed him the report and waited for his reaction.

"I've seen a few autopsies. And if this is a forgery, it's a good one. It does say she died of poisoning. If it had been an overdose of prescribed or even illegal drugs, they wouldn't have used this kind of language. This is a preliminary report, so there'd be a follow-up with tests. They may have done that by now. Anyway, it looks legit."

"Why would someone give this to Chuck?"

"To a lot of people in the police bureaucracy, Chuck's the only reporter they actually know. So if you want to disclose something to the press, he'd be the one you'd think of. We think of him as kind of a low-level guy, but to people in that world, he's their muckraker. As far as quitting goes," he shrugged, "you may not have noticed because you're not in the newsroom much, but people are quitting every day. It hasn't been a fun place to work in a long time. Nobody's gotten a raise and rumor is they're thinking about cutting everybody's pay, maybe by ten percent. The only reason there's anyone left besides Fred and June is most can't find another job."

"Yeah, guess I hadn't realized it was that bad. So, all my suspicions could just be in my head?"

"Could be. Or not. Don't get me wrong; Chuck's weird. But what he gave you just isn't conclusive. If it was me, I'd give that autopsy to Fred, and let him and the legal eagles figure it out. Also, I figure Fred will order me—since Chuck's gone—to see if there's any new information on Janet Knight's death. He'd consider it hard news, not something for you. So you could hold on to it, but you run the risk of something happening and you looking bad for not sharing. Or you toss it to your boss and let him handle it." Vince crossed his arms.

He was right. Tommy had let Albright's paranoia spook him. "Okay. First thing tomorrow, I'll go see Fred and give him my little time-bomb for him to worry about. Thanks."

"Sure. Look, I need to get going so I don't upset the family. You take care, okay?"

"I will. See ya." Vince left. Tommy was already thinking about Patsy and was about to leave when Steve Marsh approached.

"Got just a second?" He seemed sober, and uneasy.

"I guess." Tommy sat back down.

"Okay, so you and I haven't exactly been friends. I was wrong about some of that shit, but you also know those asshole tough guys of Albright's shouldn't have done what they did. Anyway, there's no reason for you and me to be fighting." Tommy noticed he seemed jumpy, fearful of something or someone. "We need to talk, but not now. I'll call you."

"Yeah. That's fine. Look, I never wanted to fight with you. So we're good." Tommy wanted to leave, too.

"Yeah, yeah, we're fine. Okay, gotta go."

Marsh left by the back door. Tommy stayed a moment, trying to figure out what that had been about.

"What was wrong with him?" Larry Lopez asked.

"Not sure. He seemed sober, but kind of out of his mind or something. Not sure I should've let him leave." Tommy shrugged.

Larry headed to the back parking lot. "I'm just going to check and see if he got out of here okay."

Tommy left. He was tired of paranoid questions and weird encounters. He wanted nothing other than to be with Patsy.

The phone rang just as they got into the bedroom. "Shit."

"Don't answer."

"I don't want to, but it could be important."

Patsy cocked a hip. "Am I not important?" There was no contest—the phone went unanswered.

Later, while Tommy fixed late-night scrambled eggs, the phone rang again. Patsy was asleep. He answered. "Hello."

"It's Louongo. Steve Marsh tried to kill Max and Nathan. Steve had the hospital call me. He's hurt bad and in intensive care. Max and Nathan called me, too; said they were walking to Albright's from Triple's when Marsh tried to run them down. They jumped out of the way, and he ran into a tree. He hit his head, and he's in bad shape. He's over at Saint Anthony, going in and out of consciousness. The guys took off before the cops got there, so the official story is Steve was drunk and rammed a tree. The doctors say he might not make it through the night. And that he wants to see you."

"Me?"

"Yeah. They say he wants to tell you about somebody named Chuck. Does that mean anything to you? They say he said, 'Chuck has to be stopped.'"

"I'll be right there."

Tommy wrote a note to Patsy, hoping that she wouldn't be too pissed, got into his clothes and headed out. *Chuck has to be stopped.* Tommy felt angry with Marsh, Max, Nathan and especially Louongo, who'd acted before like he hardly knew Marsh. But now, on his deathbed, the guy calls Louongo? *Is everybody a liar?*

Tommy got off the hospital elevator and spotted Louongo in a chair, his head in his hands.

"Too late, Tommy. He died." He seemed wrung out. He didn't get up or look directly at him.

"I'm sorry. He was a friend?"

"In the past. We used to be great drinkin' buddies. We had some pretty wild times. Once he became a big-time sports-writer, he kind of shunned me. I was just some ambulance-chasing hustler, and he was a star. But when he really needed a friend, usually late at night, he'd call me."

"This stuff about Chuck. Do you know anything?"

"No. I don't know any Chuck. It sounded kinda crazy. Maybe it was just his damaged brain making shit up, I don't know. Sorry I bothered you."

"Hey, it's okay. How about some coffee?"

"Nah, I'm goin' home. You should, too. Thanks for coming down." Louongo got up and trudged to the far exit. Tommy thought about what happened. It was late, but he decided to call Albright anyway.

"Yeah, what the hell is this about?"

"Taylor—"Tommy started.

"Yeah, who the hell is this?" Albright interrupted irritably.

"It's Tommy. Louongo called me about Steve Marsh. He was in an accident, got taken to Saint Anthony's. He asked Louongo to call me to get me down there. Before I could talk to him, he died. Louongo was upset and just left. He said Marsh tried to run down Max and Nathan."

Long silence. Maybe Albright had trouble gathering his thoughts. "Why did he want to see you?"

"He told Louongo that someone named Chuck needed to be stopped. Louongo didn't know who he was talking about. I think I do."

❧

In a conference room sat four officers who'd handled the investigation of a body found on the base. They were waiting for General Langston. Langston came in, his executive officer with him. "Gentlemen, what do you have for me?"

Colonel Pete Noble began. "We have something of a mess on our hands, sir. We know Staff Sergeant Milton was killed off-base, and his body was brought in. That creates some legal issues regarding jurisdiction and civilian responsibility. As I've discussed with you previously, we're not getting the type of cooperation we'd like from the police department. Chief Underwood has been openly hostile toward our requests for meetings to discuss it. The last time I talked to him, I told him it appeared Milton was murdered in Oklahoma City, and therefore the act was within their jurisdiction. He said," the Colonel referred to his notes, "'Fuck you and the whole goddamn Air Force, can't you just handle your own shit?'" Noble looked at the general. "We think our next approach should be to the state police, but that's one of the things we'd like to decide during this meeting."

"Do we know why he was killed? Are there any suspects? Also, any idea why the body was brought to the base? That's what really troubles me."

Major Collins, who had primary responsibility for the investigation, cleared his throat. "We're sure the murder is tied to the smuggling of drugs from South America. We believe Sergeant Milton was working with someone off base in a criminal enterprise. Our prime suspect for his accomplice is a former airman named Chuck Branson. After he left the Air Force, he worked for the base paper a while, then ended up as a police beat reporter for the *OK Journal*. We believe that while there he came into contact with one Frank Martin, who ran a large organized crime operation out of the stockyards in Oklahoma City, which included distribution of illegal drugs in Oklahoma and Texas."

"Do we know where Branson and Martin are currently?"

"It appears Martin has left the country. Branson was being followed up to a couple of days ago, but he spotted us and has gone underground."

"What have we shared with police?"

"Nothing, sir. That would have posed a problem. Branson had a lot of contacts within the police department, possibly including the chief, so we weren't comfortable with giving them anything substantial. Their potential involvement is part of what's complicating this whole matter."

"Shit, what a mess." The general would have preferred air combat to this kind of crap. "We've got to get some civilian authorities involved before it ends up looking like we tried to cover this up. What do you suggest?" He threw the question to everyone.

Colonel Noble jumped in. "We think it has to be federal— FBI, the drug agency, maybe customs. Approach it from the smuggling side. The state police are an option, but we think we should hold off on that because it could easily turn into a shouting match between the state and the city, and we'd just be caught in the middle."

"Have any federal agencies been contacted?"

"No, sir. Waiting for your approval."

"One more item. Are our planes still being used to smuggle the drugs?"

"No, sir. We've arrested three other airmen who'd worked

with Milton. All procedures regarding cargo and tracking the shipments have been changed, with improved controls. We've stopped the pipeline. As a matter of fact, we suspect that may have been why Milton was killed. Our investigators may have done something to tip off the parties that they were close to being caught, so he was eliminated to stop any connection with the off-base elements."

Langston was still puzzled. "But why bring the body back to the base?"

"Just a guess, sir, but we think it might have been to keep it away from the police department. But maybe more than that, to keep it away from the press."

"So, our policy of giving minimal information to the press was used against us. We'll need to re-evaluate that—right, Lieutenant Davis?"

"Yes, sir." Davis didn't look happy.

OK Journal

My View—Tommy Jacks

Steve Marsh was a competitor, in more ways than one. Yes, he led the Sooners to a national championship some years ago, and if you don't know the details, then you're probably the only attentive being in Oklahoma that doesn't. But he also competed in newspapers, and if you don't know how, then you must have just arrived in town from a distant galaxy.

It would be a bit of a fib to say I never ran across him, even if our professional paths didn't coincide. In fact, Steve kept popping up in different parts of my beat. As you'll read elsewhere, he worked as a sportswriter for the *Oklahoma Sun*. I hope no explanation for the difference in our jobs is necessary. Covering sports may be a lot like covering politics and vice versa, but the players can be different. He didn't spend much time at the capitol, and I can't recall the last time I stepped foot anywhere near Owen Field.

We knew each other, but we weren't friends. But I wasn't his enemy, nor was he mine. When I'd heard he'd been in an accident and later died, it felt like the world we'd both worked in turned a little smaller, a little darker, and more dangerous, although it's hard to tell how much.

There is controversy over why Steve drove his car into a tree harder than any defensive tackle ever hit him. Some say he must have been drunk. The simplest explanation always seems best, but that only works if everything else about a situation is simple. And it's not.

Steve wrote columns mainly about OU and Big Eight football, and I write mine about the contact sport that is government in this state, but neither are simple. Politics and sports connect to the out-of-sight power plays in this state, each part of a fiendishly complex game. The stakes are high, and getting higher. And chances are Steve didn't fold. My money says he got dealt out. And you can trust Chief Walter Underwood and his squad of—let's just call them police until we figure out what they really are—not to tell the truth about what happened to him. That's been their modus operandi up to now.

23

NEW IS OLD AND OLD IS NEW

Coverage of Steve Marsh's death was extensive, almost like with the passing of J.H. Gilmore. Radio and television aired exhaustive special reports. Some sportscasters grumbled about the lack of response by the Oklahoma City Police Department and directed editorial anger at Chief Underwood. Some believed toxicology reports wouldn't back up the notion that Marsh had been drinking; others speculated he'd been murdered. There was no obvious reason for anyone to kill him. Still, that didn't stop the opinion machine.

Both papers gave the matter in-depth coverage. The *Sun* ran a spread memorializing his life in sports and as a writer, with quotes from ex-players and coaches as well as fellow journalists. Everyone was shocked. The grief was real. Readers and fans would miss Steve Marsh.

Tracy was upset, too. She had dated him, and at times the relationship had been serious. But there was always one issue that drove them apart: his addiction to prescription drugs. She saw how they turned his life into a roller coaster of emotions, one day the normal Steve Marsh and a monster the next. She knew it was from his playing days. He'd told her half the team was taking something supplied by one of the equipment guys. He said without the drugs, he could never have withstood the pain of playing. After he stopped playing and started writing about it, he had no trouble finding a doctor who would write a prescription in exchange for tickets to a big game. She'd never told anyone because she didn't want to hurt him, but she kept her distance. She was convinced it would eventually kill him and didn't want to watch.

Tracy was in her first week back at KVY, where the news manager gushed about how good she was and about positive comments from the audience. She was one of three co-hosts for a part-news, part-gossip show called "AM Oklahoma." It was immediately apparent her two co-hosts were morons who did or said whatever they were told. She handled all the news, as well as interviews that involved serious issues. Her co-hosts baked cookies and talked weather and sports. Back in the field, Tracy used to complain about the happy-talk hacks at the studio. Now she was one.

"Morning, Tracy. You look great. And the last couple of shows have been fantastic. I thought it would take you some time to get use to this, but you've nailed it every day." More gushing from producer Tony Adams. "You probably think I'm just blowin' smoke, but we're getting hundreds of calls from viewers raving about you and how much better you've made the show. Congratulations!"

Tracy almost rolled her eyes but caught herself. "Thanks, Tony. I appreciate the kind words."

"I've already told the station manager we've got to have you on the air more. The viewers want you. So, get ready—we're going to make you a big star. What I want to start is a daily segment where you interview someone from the non-entertainment world. We can let Cathy and Rich interview all the movie stars, but for you we'll do something totally different. You'll interview local businessmen, politicians, professionals— you know, normal people. Won't that be great?"

Tracy put on her best movie-star smile. "That's brilliant, Tony." She felt like she might puke. She would give this nonsense another month. If it kept up like this, she'd soon be unemployed again.

Ray was greeted warmly by his new staff, except perhaps for Mike Sanders. He seemed a little cool. Most were reporters with some connection to politics, so Ray was a known entity to them. Some of the younger ones got the quick and dirty version of his story from their peers. At their first staff meeting, Ray was annoyed by one guy in particular who only seemed interested in hearing about Ray's time at Big Mac, or the more common name prison.

Also, while the group, judging by their resumes and experience, should have been well-educated, Ray was shocked at how little they knew. He proposed a series of articles to concentrate on the bills most likely to get to the floors of the Senate and House in the next session. He suggested an approach based on analyzing the bills and the impacts they would have on various segments of the population. He mostly got blank stares.

One of the brighter members of the group at the table offered his insight. "Guess you don't know this, but the staffs of the legislative leaders give us a summary of the bills before the session. They tell us right in there the impact those laws will have if they're passed. So, we just use that." The guy looked smug, like he'd been helpful to someone who was a little behind the times.

Ray could tell he wasn't getting through. "Let's suppose what they give you is complete bullshit. How would you know?" They thought he was dense, that he didn't understand how things worked. He was making their jobs harder, while the way they handled things was easy. Why rock the boat?

Tommy's plan had been to dump Janet Knight's autopsy into Fred's lap and go on about his day. After the previous night's visit to the hospital, he wasn't so sure. He was sure Steve Marsh's dying warning was about Chuck Branson. It couldn't be a coincidence. Now he had more circumstantial evidence Chuck was involved in something, though still no clue as to what. Of course, Chuck's disappearance could be explained: he quit and left, end of story. Tommy didn't think so. He decided on a plan that made him feel distinctly uncomfortable. He would go to police headquarters and ask questions.

Walking up to the information window in the lobby, Tommy was fighting a terrible sense of déjà vu. The guy behind the protective glass was the same one who called for reinforcements the last time he asked a question.

"I'd like to speak to someone who could give me some of the latest crime statistics." He smiled. Maybe the guy wouldn't recognize him.

"You're that damn reporter—the guy who made a big scene in here. You know, I got my ass reamed really good because of you." The clerk looked angry, but dialed the phone. Covering the phone, he asked in his angry voice, "What's your name?"

"Tommy Jacks, *OK Journal*."

The guy talked and listened. "You can go up. Go to the fifth floor and tell the receptionist you want to see a Captain Burke." He continued to give Tommy ugly looks. They didn't hurt much, so far.

"Thanks for seeing me, Captain Burke."

"What can I do for you?"

Tommy felt like he'd fallen into another universe. The cop was actually smiling. "I'm working on a story about the recent increase in crime." He wasn't. He was just fishing. "I was wondering if the department had any numbers you could share." Tommy had on his "you can trust me" face.

"Yeah, we're tracking that, too. You know, it's mostly just the increased drug traffic and of course the overdose deaths we're most worried about. We had the high-profile murder of that ballplayer, but those don't drive our numbers up much."

"I'd heard about those overdoses." He hadn't. "What can you tell me?"

"The whole country's seeing an increase in drug crime. I think it's the damn hippies and their influence. Need to round up every one of them, cut their damn hair and send them to 'Nam." The smile was replaced by a scowl.

"Yeah, it's a little out of hand. But I would've thought that was mostly in California."

"Well, yeah, but we've had our share. We've had some known druggies who overdosed and died. But we think the supplier is delivering stronger drugs, or they're less diluted than these people are used to. So, they shoot their normal amount, and, pow! Dead."

"Why would the drugs be stronger?"

"Not sure. Maybe somebody doesn't know what they're doing, like not cutting the stuff right. It's not like they have to worry about customer complaints." He thought that was funny.

Tommy talked a little more with the cooperative captain, who said his job was keeping track of crime statistics and reporting them to the FBI. He complained the current chief, Underwood, wasn't interested in numbers. Tommy got the feeling he was so talkative because usually no one talked to him.

"I'm hearing rumors this drug business is somehow connected with Tinker. Do you know anything about that?"

"Nah. I just collect data. Any ongoing investigation would be the detectives, upstairs. I track what's already happened. Don't know shit about what's going on up there." The friendly cop had returned.

Tommy thanked Captain Burke and left. His first thought was to head to Denny's to see if Albright was still there. He remembered he'd soon be headed back to New York, which gave him a sinking feeling. He was going to miss him a lot.

The early morning rush was over at Denny's. Tommy found Albright in all his glory, surrounded by newspapers and flanked by Max and Nathan, both looking extra sharp. It crossed Tommy's mind that the bodyguards must get up at dawn to look so put-together at such an hour.

"Good morning." Tommy was pleased to see them all. Maybe Albright had changed his mind about leaving.

"Morning, Tommy." Albright seemed troubled but upbeat.

"Glad you guys weren't hurt," he told Max and Nathan, who also looked a little solemn.

"Yeah, we were never at much risk," Max answered for them. "Marsh had to be on something, the way he was driving. Anyone who wasn't smashed could have avoided that tree. He'd decided we were his enemy, which of course, we weren't. Feel badly that he died. We went to the car after he hit the tree. Looked like he had serious head injuries, so all we could do was call the cops and an ambulance. We thought it was best if we just disappeared."

"Glad you came by, Tommy," Albright put in. "If you hadn't, I was going to call. Our plane leaves in a few hours, and we're officially out of here. What you said about Chuck is very troubling. I thought about it a lot last night and this morning. Somehow this all ties together with Dealin' Dave, his little brother, and T.D. McFadden. Those guys wouldn't know shit about taking over a crime business from Frank Martin. That never made any sense. But if Chuck had been working with Martin, he would have been a natural to take the reins. Why he might need those other guys, I don't know. Maybe just as a front. If that's true, Chuck is one dangerous guy. You need to be extra careful. Remember, he knows you and no doubt he knows the trouble you can cause. You should pull in your horns and let someone else handle Chuck." Albright frowned.

"Yeah, maybe. I can tell you I feel a lot more vulnerable with you guys leaving town."

"You need to keep writing, but you have to reduce your risk. I'd recommend you talk to your dad, maybe move in with him and Tracy for a few weeks. You've got yourself in a bind with the police and Underwood. I've got a name for you, going all the way back to my Dartmouth days. This one guy ended up in Washington and moved up quickly in the FBI. I talked to him this morning, and he's willing to help. He gave me a name here in the Oklahoma City office." Albright slid a piece of paper with a name and number to Tommy. "Give him a call."

"Also, Tommy," Max said, leaning forward with a grim look. "You need to be ready. If this starts to get out of hand, jump on a plane. There'll always be a place for you in New York City." He gave Tommy another piece of paper with another phone number.

OK Journal

My View—Tommy Jacks

Remember that long article last year about two guys who looked like hippies, and didn't much deny that they were, passing through our pristine state? They got stopped, detained, pulled off a series of buses, and told to cool their heels in the lobbies of police stations from Pryor to Oklahoma City to Clinton and Erick. They saw the back seats of more police cruisers than official police cruiser backseat inspectors, all because they looked like hippies, and wouldn't say they weren't. Remember?

Ewell Knight and Roger Bidwell, by name, were just trying to get from Minnesota to California, and boy, did they take a wrong turn. They were searched every ten miles, by even a casual calculation. The strongest chemical matter found on either was

aftershave lotion, which was confiscated and taken to a lab, which sent back results—yep, Aqua Velva, all right.

To date, that's pretty much the extent of what's been done in this state vis-à-vis hippies and suspicious chemicals. There's nothing so far to implicate them in the matter of illegally transporting illicit narcotics into our fair state. But according to a source, hippies are to blame for the presence of these drugs—which are not only unlawful, but deadly—on our streets.

Mind you, the source doesn't know that for sure. But here's what a conversation with that source has revealed.

First, that an influx of such drugs has found its way into the state.

Second, that those drugs

are deadly because they are far stronger than what most addicts are used to. That means they not only can kill addicts, they can also be fatal to people who shoot them up for the first time.

Third, that deaths by overdose are, as a result, going up.

The source has the numbers on all these, but no specific facts as to who is bringing them in and just assumes they are "hippies," which we all know is kind of an umbrella term for everyone who disagrees with the prevailing political outlook as put forth by, say, U.S. Attorney General John Mitchell. Mitchell yesterday swore during a Law Day speech at Harvard University that such people should be dealt with severely. He's convinced they're the cause of campus unrest, and by extension, of more general civil unrest. And drugs, he and the source believe, are part of the hippie plot to undermine America.

"I call for an end to minority tyranny on the nation's campuses," he thundered at Harvard. "It is not an admission of defeat, as some say, to use reasonable physical force to eliminate physical force."

Compare that to what my source about the drug crime said: "I think it's the damn hippies and their influence. Need to round up every one of them and cut their damn hair and send them to 'Nam."

So a killer is stalking our streets, and unrest is threatening our nation, and the best we can do is identify as the culprit a class of people we as a society find it hard to identify with. These days are getting darker. ❧

24
MEETING OF THE MINDS

They decided on lunch at The Petroleum Club, a more or less neutral spot. It was a downtown institution where many private meetings were held, for good and ill. It was more Gilmore's turf than Anderson's. Bill insisted on a private room. Their chosen hour of two was deliberate to avoid any accidental encounters and incidental rumors. Bill arrived a little early, punctual to a fault. Robbie Gilmore was notoriously late for everything, always rushed. Today was no exception, even if the club was close to his office.

Bill sat in the swank private dining room, which was suitable for twelve but set up for two. It guaranteed maximum privacy. He ordered sweet iced tea. He wasn't sure what to think about Robbie. He wasn't his father, head of the Gilmore publishing empire for decades and the force behind the vicious gubernatorial campaign that caused Bill so much anguish. Still, not being J.H. Gilmore didn't necessarily make him a man you could trust.

Robbie arrived, requested a gin martini, and seated himself across the table. Neither offered to shake hands. "Sorry I'm a little late. I'm only a few blocks away and should've walked. They had some water issues and had Broadway blocked, so it took me a bit longer than I'd expected." He smiled, but it didn't seem friendly.

"You know, I guess we've never met," Bill said. "I met your father several times at some social things. Do you mind if I call you Robbie, or do you prefer something else?"

"Sorry. Sometimes I forget my manners. Yes, please. And you, is it Bill?"

"Yes. Only my mother calls me William." Both relaxed a little. "Your paper lied about me and my positions, and no doubt caused me to lose the election." Bill made the flat statement with little expression.

"Well, I don't know that we lied. It was a tough race, and sometimes those things can lead to some less than accurate information being tossed about." If Robbie was offended, he didn't show it.

Bill chuckled. "You don't understand. I meant to thank you. I realized toward the end of the campaign that I really didn't want to be a governor. You and your dad saved me four years of absolute hell." He wasn't known for his sense of humor.

Robbie smiled through a quiet pause. "My dad was very bitter toward almost everything in his last years. He wanted to win at all costs, no matter who got hurt. He had few friends at the end. I'm not my dad. I thought we handled the coverage of the campaign between you and Butler in a shameful manner. And if I'd been a better person, I would've told my dad that and quit. But I didn't."

"Family's a hard thing. We love 'em, and we need them more than anything, but sometimes our vision of what's right and wrong gets clouded by them." Bill reached across the table and extended his hand. Robbie looked at Bill for a second, then shook it.

"How can we make life better for ourselves and the people of Oklahoma?" Robbie spoke from a surprisingly comfortable realization that he and Bill might work together.

"For one, we could work on a way to keep both papers fighting for readership, but not for survival, while at the same time giving people the information they need to make good, informed decisions."

"Any ideas?"

Bill laid out some thoughts about how to cut costs for both papers, amounting to a proposal for a joint operating agreement. Each would stay independent, but they would cooperate to form a new company to provide printing and other services to the individual papers and to other businesses. Bill estimated that it could cut each newspaper's printing overhead by about twenty-five percent.

"Plus, it would give us the opportunity to upgrade equipment, which we need now. We both need more color and better graphics if we're going to compete with television. And in the near term, I see national papers taking away some of our market unless we're aggressive in keeping the product as new and innovative as possible."

Robbie was impressed. He'd been having internal discussions about these same matters. "Wouldn't that reduce our competitive edge—my willingness to beat your brains in, and vice versa?" Robbie offered that with a light chuckle, but it was still a good question.

"One of us could beat the other by purchasing new equipment to put out a better-looking product—on that I agree. But if we go down the path of constantly trying to outdo one another with large capital expenditures, we will drive one of us, maybe both, into bankruptcy. We should compete with every ounce of our energy on our content, our reporters, our innovations and ideas. And we would."

"Do you think this would be legal? Our laws don't exactly encourage this sort of industry cooperation."

"True. I don't have a complete answer yet. But I think protecting the First Amendment has a high value for many politicians. My guess is that either it'll turn out to be legal, or we'll be able to get some kind of exemption to antitrust laws."

They ordered their late lunch and ended up talking about racehorses.

Tommy's first call to the local office of the FBI wasn't promising. He was asked a lot of questions about why he was calling, and then he was passed to another person who asked the same questions all over again. But he didn't want to give out much until he could talk to the person whose name he'd been given.

"I know you're doing what you're supposed to do, but I was told to talk to Agent O'Connor specifically. If he's not available, I'll call back. But asking me the same questions over and over isn't going to get us anywhere, okay? I was given O'Connor's name, and that of a Special Agent Swartz in Washington. If Agent O'Connor isn't there, I can call Washington." Tommy could hear the person's breathing change at the mention of Washington. Maybe that was the key.

"Agent O'Connor, how can I help you?"

Tommy explained who he was and that he had indirectly been given his name by Special Agent Swartz in Washington. They agreed to meet at the downtown field offices on the

eighth floor of the First National Bank building. It wasn't exactly hidden, but it wasn't obvious, either. In the reception area
sat a woman behind an enclosed counter with what looked like
a little round speaker set in the glass, apparently to communicate. Except for that, it could have been an attorney's office.
Tommy spoke into the disk and told her his name. He was
asked to take a seat.

In just a few minutes, a tall and very thin man came out.
"Tommy Jacks? I'm Agent O'Connor." He showed Tommy
into a room that was bare except for a table and four chairs.
"First, you should know Special Agent Swartz is very high up
in the Washington headquarters hierarchy. So when he calls,
things start jumping. Second, we're aware of what's been going
on with the police department and the chief. I can't offer any
details." O'Connor paused to let that sink in. "In a separate
matter, I've been authorized to tell you that a task force of several agencies within the federal government has been working
with the Air Force to unscramble a mess due to Frank Martin
skipping town. It's created a race to the bottom for several of
our citizens. We'll be cleaning that up in time."

"I guess that's good. I'm not real sure you told me much
other than you expect to do something soon." Tommy was not
easily impressed by bureaucratic doublespeak.

O'Connor's voice and manner quickly turned governmental.
"By nature, we're not forthcoming. Look—you're a reporter or,
I guess, technically a columnist. We don't want to read about
ourselves in the paper. So, this will have to be off the record."

"I understand. But this is *not* off the record and I *am* a reporter. So, anything you tell me could end up in the paper."
Tommy got his back up when confronted with the authoritar-

ian approach. Any sense of cooperation was gone.

"I guess I thought you were asking for our protection. If you want that, you'll have to agree not to write about any of this." Any pretense of civil discourse was gone, too. *Want us to save your ass? Keep your stupid mouth shut!*

Tommy got up, gave O'Connor his best "fuck-you" glare, and left. He knew they couldn't arrest him for treating them like the jerks they were. Still, he didn't feel comfortable until he was on the street.

So much for that idea. He felt alone. He needed to talk to someone who could give him some straight advice without the calculated doublespeak of the FBI or the "I have no idea what to do" he would get from Fred or June. He headed to Louongo's office. The man definitely had his faults, but not speaking his mind wasn't one of them.

The lawyer was in, and he was drunk. Tommy had never seen him in that state, and it made him realize Louongo had been something like background noise in his world, always present and an integral part of things. But Tommy hadn't given much thought to who he actually was.

"Well, shit, if it isn't good old Tommy Jacks. Want a drink?"

"Maybe later." Should he even try to talk to him, or just let him stew in misery? He decided the guy was probably a wise drunk, and if so, this was an opportunity. Tommy told him the whole story, as best he understood, of Chuck Branson, Frank Martin, the Harris brothers, and T.D. McFadden. "What do you think?"

Louongo had given the impression of at least listening. "Sonofabitch, that's really something. So, Martin leaves because he thinks the Air Force is getting too close, and your ex-coworker, Chuck, is now the kingpin. And for reasons nobody knows, he recruits local business people to help him keep the good times rolling. I like it. It's complete bullshit, but I like it!"

"Why is it complete bullshit?"

"Too many fuckin' moving parts. How did Chuck know those business people? What'd he do, run an ad? *Looking for gangster partners. You provide the capital; I'll provide the crime.* Doesn't make sense. And he worked quiet as a mouse at the paper for years while he accumulated tons of money—why?"

Geez, he was right. How did all that fit together? How did they find each other? And, more important, why would they just suddenly trust one another?

"You're right. It's nonsense." Tommy felt deflated. He found Louongo's liquor supply and poured a gin and tonic, no ice.

"Bottoms up." Louongo drained his drink and fixed another. "Now, your theory may not be completely wrong. It's just not right."

"How so?"

Louongo smiled. "There has to be someone else."

25
JUSTICE WILL BE DONE

Jackie Carter had been sitting in her car across the street from police headquarters for hours. She had decided to leave her hotel room and drive to the emergency room because something wasn't right. She'd coughed up blood and was having trouble standing. But on the way to Saint Anthony's, she passed police headquarters, and on impulse she pulled into an open parking spot. The longer she sat, the more convinced she became that she wouldn't live much longer. Her anger blinded her to everything else.

She was livid. She had to kill him.

Upstairs, Underwood knew he didn't have much time. One of his old pals in the state police had called to warn him the FBI was snooping around. He said he'd heard from his captain that Oklahoma City's police chief was about to be taken in, maybe the next day, and he'd heard that yesterday. Now a couple of his guys in vice just told him their division lieutenant had been contacted by the FBI. Underwood could smell his own fear.

He pulled a number out of his wallet and called. "I need a way to get out of the goddamn country—now!" he hissed into the phone.

The voice that answered sounded only slightly agitated.

"Calm down, Walter. If you panic, you'll just make things worse. You've had a good run, so now you need to be smart. Did you move the cash like I told you?"

"Yeah, it's out of the country. But *I'm* still here. Fuck."

"Walter, go to Wiley Post. Take a cab. There'll be a blue-and-gold, twin-engine Cessna. Get on it. The pilots will be waiting. They don't know a thing about you, so just keep your mouth shut. You won't even need your passport; there'll be a form you can sign to get you into Mexico as a tourist. And there'll be a change of clothes for you. You'll be in the air in minutes, to Juarez. Just keep your mouth shut, and once you're there, go to the Hotel Rio Bravo. You'll be contacted and given directions on how to get to Trinidad. Stay calm, and this'll be okay. Leave in about an hour."

"Okay. This better work."

Or what? the person on the other end of the line thought. The chief was an idiot and would have to be taken care of. *No worries—Martin would deal with him.*

Underwood paced nervously in his office. It had only been thirty minutes, but he couldn't wait. He told his secretary he had a meeting with the mayor and to call a cab so he wouldn't have to park his car. It sounded a little unusual, but she shrugged and made the call. A few minutes later her voice crackled on the intercom.

"Sir, your cab is waiting out front."

Chief Underwood got up and left. Outside he spotted the cab and headed across the street. Out of the corner of his eye he caught movement. "Shit!"

Jackie Carter shot Chief Underwood six times, spending every bullet she had. She would have reloaded and fired more, but she was tackled by three big police officers. One kicked her repeatedly. An autopsy would show he ruptured her already damaged kidney, causing massive internal bleeding and her death.

Deputy Chief Tom Lawson was named interim police chief within hours of Underwood's murder. Almost immediately, several officers came forward to say they were willing to testify to illegal activities by the chief's goon squad. The deputy chief had always held suspicions about the group, but up to this point had no evidence. He immediately arrested and charged six officers from vice. He rewrote the internal department structure to put his own people in key positions. Before anything else could be done, five other police officers left the building and disappeared.

The FBI sent a team to meet with Lawson, who they knew hadn't been involved in Underwood's operations. The attorney general's office provided a special team to collect data related to the late chief's acts over several years. As part of the investigation, a team went to Jackie Carter's hotel room and found a trove of incriminating documents that detailed the depth of the chief's corruption.

Lawson leaked many of those documents to both papers. He knew he had to conclusively prove Underwood's guilt and attempt to establish the fact that his corruption would be a thing of the past. That was necessary if he was to have any chance of cleaning up the department, especially because he would have to recruit new, honest officers.

"Press room, Tommy Jacks."

"This is Police Chief Tom Lawson. I'm glad I could reach you, Mister Jacks. The Oklahoma City Police Department owes you an apology, which I want to extend personally, for all of the things done to you under Chief Underwood. I didn't know the full extent of it back then, but I should've done a better job of monitoring what was going on and the harm that was being caused. Please accept my apology on behalf of the entire department."

Tommy was stunned. He'd heard the police chief had been shot by his former lover, but he sure as hell didn't expect a personal phone call from the new one. "Eh, yeah. Thanks. I guess a couple of times I thought I might get killed, so I'm glad that's over."

"Mister Jacks, it's all on us. I have tremendous respect for the press, and you should never have been treated like you were. Like I said, I'm just learning how bad it was. When this all gets settled, I'd like very much to give you an exclusive interview on the things I plan to do to make this department more responsive to our citizens. And as part of that, there's going to be a new approach to dealing with the press. Is that agreeable?"

"Sounds good to me, Chief."

Underwood's death and the coverage of his reign of corruption created a political firestorm. People wanted answers from the mayor, the city council, the city attorney, the attorney general, and even the governor. How could such a situation exist for so long with a thoroughly corrupt official in a major post in city government? Story after story focused on the level and scale of it. It wasn't just about fixing parking tickets. The TV stations in particular reported extensively on the cost of maintaining Underwood's mansion and the staff it required, much of it at public expense one way or another. The chief never so much as tried to hide his wealth, a fact that made it seem yet more incredible that he'd never been investigated. He had held vastly expensive parties at his mansion, with guest lists including every major player in city and state politics. One TV station estimated the cost of the parties alone exceeded Underwood's official salary by a factor of twenty. Tommy and his columns were often mentioned as an exception to the silence that had generally surrounded the chief, and many other reporters and their papers were questioned about why they ignored such an obvious matter. Of course, the TV stations questioned the newspapers, and the newspapers derided the TV stations. Everyone pointed a finger elsewhere, insisting someone else should have been a better watchdog.

"Hey, Tommy, you're getting some good press. Seems like you were just about the only guy who noticed our dead police chief was living like a king. Good job." Bart tossed out that comment as a greeting while Tommy passed him in the almost vacant halls of the capitol.

"Thanks, Bart." Tommy hadn't been pleased to be singled out. Damn near every other member of the press seemed to resent him. He had made his way back to the press room but stopped at the door. "Patsy. What are you doing here?"

"I came to rescue you. I've been calling, but your communications team seems to have left their posts. Although I did talk to June. She told me you need some watching after. So here I am, ready for watching duty. Get your stuff together—we're leaving." She crossed her arms in a way that said she wouldn't put up with resistance.

He grabbed his stuff and followed her out, willingly. "Where are we headed?"

"First to Tracy and your dad's. I called Tracy when I couldn't find you, and she said I had to bring you by so she could give you a good scolding. I thought that sounded reasonable, so that'll be our first stop."

"Okay. Then what?"

"We'll see. It'll depend on how nice you are."

They left his theft-proof ride in the capitol parking lot, taking her much nicer car instead. He began to feel almost normal after so much death had put him in a dark mood. He knew none of it was his fault, but too many people he knew or had written about were dead. Even Chief Underwood's murder saddened him. And he had to wonder about Jackie Carter and how she had to have suffered at Underwood's hands. It wasn't the first time it crossed his mind that being a reporter wasn't the world's cheeriest job. He glanced over at his beautiful Patsy White and smiled in spite of everything. He was in love, and he'd been ignoring her on account of his job. How stupid could he be?

When they arrived, his informal stepmom was waiting on the front porch, and Tommy could see a serious scolding in his future. Tracy and Patsy had talked by phone, but never actually met. Nonetheless, they greeted each other with a hug, and with that ease that seems to exist only among women.

"You are so lovely." Tracy was still holding Patsy's hand. "Please go inside—there's some tea on the table, just help yourself. We'll be right in." They exchanged a look that conveyed a great deal without saying anything else.

"Okay, I haven't been by, I'm sorry." Tommy meant it. As soon as he saw Tracy, he felt better about his life and his world.

"Albright called your dad. He was worried sick about you. You didn't tell us what was going on, and that is just plain wrong. We're your family, and if you need help, you come here. What were you thinking?" Tracy was only slightly angry, but Tommy could see she was hurt. He felt badly.

"Everything was happening so fast, I'm not sure I *was* thinking. That was my plan, to come here and stay a while until things got straightened out. Sorry if I worried you and dad. But I think most of the danger's over." Tommy lowered his head a little.

Tracy gave him a hug. "Patsy's wonderful. She's beautiful and smart. You're one lucky young man. She cares about you, and I like her a lot." Tracy gave him a look that all but ordered him to pay close attention. "You need to be more careful and keep us close." They went inside, hand in hand.

"Where's dad?"

"On his way. Lots of stuff going on at the paper, you know." Another little dig. They found Patsy in the living room. "Any chance you play Monopoly, Patsy?"

Tommy shook his head at Patsy, trying not to be noticed while he did, but Tracy spotted it. They all laughed. Patsy confessed, "Tommy already warned me that you play a very competitive game."

Tommy changed the subject. "What's going on with your show? Seems like you've become a star." He wasn't surprised. He'd heard a lot of people comment on how naturally she fit into the show.

"Yeah, it's gone okay so far. Lots more entertainment than news, so there's been some adjustment. The producer is a super hyper kind of guy who can really get on your nerves. He seems to think everything he does is new. The latest 'new' idea he has is that on certain high-profile stories he wants to send me out with a crew to cover the action on the scene. I don't believe it actually crossed his mind that that's what I did before. He thinks he's a genius for thinking it up." Tracy smiled, but there was worry behind it.

Ray arrived and gushed over Patsy. She was more than simply beautiful—people seemed to like her open, friendly manner and her way of making people feel comfortable around her. Ray paid more attention to her than to his son, but that just made Tommy proud—and feeling genuinely lucky.

After a minute, Ray broke into the small conversations to call for attention. "We have news for you. Tracy has said yes—we're getting married." The smile on his dad's face reminded Tommy of the day Ray was released from prison: complete joy.

Tracy shook her head slightly. "Your father is the worst secret-keeper I've ever met."

Tommy spent time talking to his dad about recent events while Tracy and Patsy prepared dinner. A home and a family. It was all Tommy had ever wanted.

OK Journal

My View—Tommy Jacks

The streets run red with the wrong people's blood.

It seemed too quick and too easy. In less than 60 seconds yesterday morning, Walter Underwood, up to that moment the longtime and nearly legendary chief of the Oklahoma City Police, took six .38-caliber slugs the way nobody wants to. The woman who put them there had been his right-hand person at the department, one Jackie Carter. Some cops in the vicinity with quick feet made sure she'd be as dead as the chief was.

A lot of people now think the problem is solved, a big part of it being, according to most, that the chief's mansion and after-hours indulgences overmatched his paycheck by a lot. To others, the issue seems to be that the police should now get back to policing, and they're reassured that the new chief, Tom Lawson, seems to be on that detail.

But that's too quick, too easy. We told you a few columns ago that there was more to it—a depressing, scary, heck of a lot more. Gunning down Underwood couldn't take care of it.

Documents found about the disheveled hotel room Carter rented, where she'd stayed just before she plugged Underwood and then was gang-tackled and stomped to jelly by about a half-dozen cops, only begin to connect the chief and an undetermined number of his hand-picked vice patrol officers to the hellfire pipeline of supercharged heroin that hit the streets months ago. It's been killing junkies and first-timers like Raid kills cockroaches.

There's a lot more to go through, and all of it promises to be ugly and dispiriting. We can say now that it was an officer in the department's data collection office—yep, the cops have one—who let us in on the numbers. But the numbers don't tell the whole story, and neither do Jackie Carter's papers. They don't tell us exactly how the cranked-up heroin got here, or who brought it or what kind of slime did the street work of selling it. They don't explain why the chief, according to a witness who saw the shooting while ducking behind a parking meter, was heading for a taxi just before Carter shot him.

He'd told his secretary he was headed to an official meeting of some sort. But, in a taxi? The man had a fleet of gassed-up cruisers. Maddeningly, the trail stops there—no names, no contacts, no threads to follow.

To get the whole story straight and quick, you'd need Under-wood. But, as has often been the case in the past, he isn't taking interviews. He's made his final and permanent appointment, and won't be back in the office.

So, it's into the depths we go. And it's going to get nauseating. Out on the street, heroin goes by another name—the same word some of us use for what we flush down the john. It's a pretty apt metaphor, maybe even too nice for what this whole business is going to smell like and look like once everything is out in the open. 🐇

26

THE GUILTY AND THE INNOCENT

Ray Jacks still felt uncomfortable walking through the news-room of the *Oklahoma Sun*. It was impossible to feel at ease after all the things he'd imagined that had gone on there. He waved to a few people and found his desk in the back. On it lay a note saying T.D. McFadden wanted him to call. The number was one he didn't recognize. That caught him off guard. What could it be about?

Mike Sanders interrupted his confusion. "Good morning, Mister Jacks."

"Hey, good morning to you, Mike. What's goin' on?"

"I've tried to call Tommy again but haven't been able to get hold of him. I feel like a fool. You know, I said some pretty stupid things to him based on what Marsh told me, and the crap Underwood's pals said, and none of it was true. I was fooled. He must think I'm a real idiot."

Ray shrugged. "Look, everybody makes mistakes. Tommy told me you apologized, so let it go. He's been involved in some misunderstandings of his own. He gets it." Ray wasn't sure about Sanders. He didn't really seem suited to this kind of work. First he flew off the handle, and then he wouldn't stop apologizing. And he hadn't produced anything at all since Ray had become his boss. "You need to concentrate on work for a while, Mike. Get some stories going, get something in the paper. I know it's hard just starting. But you're evaluated on what you write, not on whether you get along with a competing paper's political columnist."

Mike sighed. "I'm in trouble, aren't I? I knew it as soon as they hired you, I'd get fired. Is it going to happen soon?"

Ray fought the urge to punch the melodramatic sonofabitch. "Listen, Mike. Just shut up and listen. Your job is to write stories that go into the paper. If you aren't doing that, you're in trouble. So just go dig up and write stories the paper can use. Got it?"

He squirmed. "Where I was before, they had people who'd tell me what to do. Here, it's like I'm on my own. I'm not sure what to write."

Ray rubbed his face and ran his fingers though his hair, trying to think and to fight another urge to punch him. Then he wrote something on a slip of paper and handed it to Mike. "One of the representatives for Oklahoma County is T.D. Mc-Fadden. He's also in the insurance business, and he has some car lots. That's his office address. I want you to go there and ask to interview him. Can you do that?"

"Sure. If he says yes, was there something in particular I should ask him about?"

"Just ask him what his legislative goals are for next session. Take notes and come back here and write up your interview and give it to me, okay?"

"Sure, great. I'm on it." Mike left. Ray still wanted to hit him. He shook his head to get rid of the thought.

Ray called the number.

"McFadden."

"What the hell's going on, T.D.?"

"Ray. Why in hell did you quit?"

"I think *you* better tell me what this is all about first. You've been missing for days. I could just as easily have called the police when I got your message. There are a lot of questions about some of your business transactions. I need to know what all that's about."

"Shit. I knew I should've told Loretta more about it all, but I was in a hurry. I just wanted to get out of there. There's nothing going on, Ray." He sighed. "Well, crap, that's not so. There's something going on, but nothing illegal. Or maybe it is, but the only person that could be upset is my wife. Damn. I've really made a mess of things."

"I have no idea what the hell you're talking about. Where are you? Whose number is this?" T.D. wasn't making much sense and Ray was getting angry.

"I'm living in an apartment out by the capitol. The number belongs to a friend of mine. Wait—shit, Ray, this is just terrible—she's not a friend. She's my lover. My wife found out and threatened to kill me. She chased me out of the house with a gun. I thought I was a goner, for sure. My god, I've never seen her so mad. She was cussin', callin' me a sonofabitch, and all the time waving around this gun that she doesn't even know how to use. Since then, I've been hiding."

Ray couldn't help smiling with relief. It wasn't money. It was just sex. "What about all those small cash deposits? They all add up to a hell of a lot of money. What was that about?"

"That was Dealin' Dave. I don't really know what the deal was. He called and said he had someone who'd buy almost anything. He said he wanted maybe fifty or more cars and would

pay top dollar. Well, I started calling. I got hold of two buddies of mine, one in Tulsa and one in Kansas City. Before he
stopped, Dealin' Dave bought more than a hundred and fifty
cars. The whole thing was over three hundred thousand dollars
in just a few months. I didn't want to tell Loretta because she's
so damned religious, I just knew she would say there had to be
somethin' wrong with the whole thing and might even call the
cops. I guess if she talked to you about the deposits, then you
saw the check. That was to the guy in Kansas City. Most of the
cars ended up coming from him, and he was so worried about
the deal not being legit, he wouldn't take cash. Said it smelled
wrong, so he insisted on a check. And that's how I paid him.
My pal in Tulsa just took cash, but it was a lot less."

"T.D., you have really screwed things up."

"Maybe so. Listen, I don't want this to sound corny to you,
okay? But I'm in love. I know my political career is over, and I
know my wife is gonna file for divorce and squeeze every dime
she can out of me. But I've never been happier."

Ray laughed a deep and genuine laugh. "Oh, by the way, I
sent one of my cub reporters to your office to get an interview.
He's new and he's a little fragile, so if you see him and have
some time, talk to him a little, okay? And hell, who knows? The
times, they are a-changing. Maybe having a girlfriend while
you're married isn't a political no-no anymore."

Several dozen agents of the FBI and the Federal Bureau of
Narcotics raided Dealin' Dave's offices. They presented search
warrants for everything, including the Harris brothers' houses,
and arrest warrants for each. Dealin' Dave's brother was listed

on his warrant as "Little Dave."

But both were waiting for them, with their attorney. There apparently was a leak somewhere. Joe Louongo stood, smiling, beside his clients. After some discussion which mostly consisted of Louongo making it very clear his clients would have nothing to say, and that they decried the overkill of using military tactics to serve warrants on innocent businessmen, the Harris brothers were escorted in handcuffs to a waiting FBI car and whisked away. Within minutes, a large contingent of TV station trucks and newspaper reporters arrived to take Louongo's statement.

"The federal police have overstepped their authority, and have arrested my clients based on fiction, on charges ranging from jaywalking to murder. I think they will soon learn that the laws of Oklahoma don't allow for this kind of abuse of civil rights. If these men have committed some offense in the state of Oklahoma, then that's something for local authorities to handle, not some secret police from the federal government. This federal intervention will not be tolerated by the free people of the state of Oklahoma."

Louongo was such a natural on TV, it was surprising he hadn't already been hired by one of the stations. When his statement was over, a small smattering of applause could be heard, mostly from the camera operators. They weren't entirely sure what he'd said, but they damn sure agreed with it.

Agent O'Connor stood several paces away, shaking his head. He'd never seen such an act. "We have no comment," was all he said when asked for his thoughts.

❦

Little Dave had met Chuck Branson months before at a bar off of 10th Street, a low-ceilinged hole in the wall. The only people who went there were lowlifes, mostly because it was a congenial and unthreatening place unless you weren't a lowlife. On that late afternoon, the drinkers were biding their time until dark, sipping their beers so they wouldn't get completely slammed before seven. Little Dave and Chuck were the only ones at the bar. Neither knew the other at the time, although Chuck knew who Little Dave was.

"I hate those fuckin' Sooners," Dave grumbled, just for something to grumble about. "All those rich assholes go up there and cheer for 'em unless they lose, and then they want somebody's head on a spike."

Chuck was not interested in football, but was interested in talking to Little Dave. "You must be a Cowboys fan."

"Yep. Now, that's a real team. Those guys get the scrubs, not those top guys from all over the country. I bet half the Cowboy team players are from Oklahoma. The damn OU team, I bet it's not ten percent from the state."

"Yeah," Chuck agreed, just to keep the ball rolling. "The whole thing's for rich people. I don't know anyone who went to either school. And our damn legislators spend tons of money on new buildings for them almost every year. My cousin lives in a shitty part of town out by Moore. Their kids go to a school that's nothing but a damn barracks the goddamn army gave 'em. Meanwhile these rich college brats are walking around in million-dollar buildings with manicured yards. I was in the Air Force for years and got my fill of crap rolling downhill. Just once, before I die, I'd like to be on top of that pile of shit." The more they talked, the more they drank. The more they drank, the more the talk edged into dangerous territory.

"Yep, it's crap. I work for my brother in his damn car lot." Little Dave shrugged, looking morose. "He's okay, but, shit. It'd be great to be the boss and tell other people what to do."

Chuck nodded to convey sympathy. "I cover all kinds of crap for the *OK Journal.* I go to crime scenes and follow up on who's been arrested, shit like that. But I know lots about the crime scene here. A buddy of mine was just killed out at Tinker because he crossed some of the big guys."

"You're shittin' me. Guy was killed?" Little Dave didn't like the sound of that. He wondered whether he should say adios to this guy.

"Yeah. But then a strange thing happened. Frank Martin— you heard of him? He was the head honcho. But he up and left town. Suddenly about half the town doesn't have an organized crime boss."

Chuck went on to lay out his idea to Little Dave about what he thought might work for guys like them. They maybe could take over the prostitution business on the west side of town. No one would care, not even the cops. But what they needed was to get their hands on some motels. He figured they could get some great deals on some places because most were vacant slums. Nobody was using them for anything, let alone prostitution.

At first Little Dave thought the guy was just blowing smoke. Now he was starting to wonder if there might be something to his ideas after all. "Havin' a place is one thing. What about the whores?"

Chuck leaned in a little closer to whisper, "I've got a list. I came across it on my day job. It's got all the whores who worked for Frank Martin. The vice cops kept it—but these guys, they'll do whatever you want as long as you pay. So they sold it to me. I think they thought I wanted it just so I could get laid, or maybe they thought I wanted to use the girls as sources. They didn't care, long as I paid for it." He looked around furtively, as if to make sure no one else was listening. "It's got nearly *a hundred names.*" That made Little Dave's eyes flash. "If we can get started before somebody else steps in, we can take over that entire business. It'd be a gold mine."

Now Little Dave was seriously interested. "What would it take?"

"Money and guts."

27
GOOD IS BETTER

Tommy walked slowly through the nearly vacant capitol, noticing the eerie quality of the building without most of its people. When it was populated, it often felt warm and inviting. Now it seemed cold and harsh. He tried to remember the feeling when he first walked into the lobby—how impressive it was, and how excited he'd felt to work in such a dynamic place. On that first day, he believed he would write about the good and the bad in government, and always focus on the consequences of the leaders' decisions on ordinary people—how this bill or that bill made life a little bit better by fixing something. He wasn't sure he'd done that. He had trouble remembering a story about any good that had gotten done. He knew there *was* good, but the bad jumped out and grabbed you and made you notice. The good was hidden and not so easy to see.

He thought of Gail in Senator Evans's office, and how many times he'd seen her helping someone, maybe just answering a question or giving directions. She was always generous with her time and never acted like she was someone important. But she was. He remembered Judy, and how she helped Bart on his first day as a security guard, making him feel like he belonged when he felt like he didn't.

In the press room, he was surprised to see Mike Sanders

with his head down on a desk. He wasn't sure if he was asleep. When Tommy walked by, he stirred. "Oh, hey. Guess I dozed off. I need your help, Tommy."

"Sure, Mike."

"Your dad sent me to interview T.D. McFadden at his business office. But he wasn't there, and they didn't seem to know when he'd be back. So I came here, but he wasn't in the office here, either. I think I'm going to get fired if I don't write something that actually makes it into the paper. Can you give me some ideas?"

Tommy gave it some thought. "First, you can't just write something. You're a reporter, and I understood that your area was politics, which is quiet right now. So you have to *find* a story. There's a couple of things you could try this morning. Go to the governor's office—there'll be people there in just a bit. Ask to speak to the governor. They'll tell you no. Ask for his agenda for the week. They might tell you he doesn't have one, or they might tell you to get lost. The important thing is, you've got to be out there looking for something, asking questions." Tommy thought about what else Mike might do. "Here's another idea. Go to Senator Evans's office and talk to Gail Collins. She's his top assistant; she's worked here forever. Just talk to her. Tell her you're doing human interest stories on the people who work at the capitol. Ask her about her best memory of working here. Just get her talking and I bet she'll give you some things you can write about. You have to go out and *look for* the story."

"Thanks. I don't know if I can do that, but I'll try." Sanders left, not looking very enthusiastic.

The press room phone rang.

"Press room. Tommy Jacks."

"Hey, how are you?" Patsy sounded concerned.

"I'm okay. Can't seem to shake the blues, though, and I'm not sure why. It sure isn't you. You're wonderful. Will you marry me?"

"No, you're still too much of a baby. I might in a year or two. If you cheer up."

"Interesting rejection." Tommy smiled, which happened a lot when he talked to Patsy.

"Maybe you miss Albright."

"Yeah, I've thought about that. Those sessions at Denny's were a lot more like therapy than anything else. Plus, and I know this is going to sound weird, the grumpier Albright was, the happier I seemed to be. It was some sort of balancing act we had. I needed to be happy because he was such a sourpuss, just to keep the world in balance. But now he's not here."

"I think you miss him because he was a great friend. That's going to take a while before it stops hurting."

"You're a smart, beautiful person. Are you sure you won't marry me?"

"Yeah, pretty sure. How about we go out tonight? Maybe go to Risso's for pizza."

"It's a date."

Tommy spent much of the day in the press room, working on some columns and putting together an agenda for the next few months. There were things he wanted to look into. Plus, he wanted to get an interview with Fred Hawkins, the other U.S. senator from Oklahoma, to get his reaction to Knight's declaration that he wasn't going to run again. And he wanted to follow up with the new police chief once he was settled in and set up the interview he'd promised. After mapping out potential projects, he started to feel better.

"Mister Jacks?"

Tommy jumped. He hadn't heard anyone come in. "Yeah, that's me." The man standing in the room was someone in charge of something; it was obvious from looking at him.

"I'm Paul Swartz. I'm a friend of Taylor Albright's." He extended his hand.

Tommy stood to shake it. "Swartz of the Washington FBI. Nice to meet you."

"I talked to Agent O'Connor. Sounds like you two didn't hit it off. I was in town, called the paper, and they said you might be here. Have a minute?"

"Sure. Have a seat."

"There are a lot of FBI agents who think the press is our enemy, and I suspect O'Connor may be one. That's not the position of the FBI, and for sure not my view. Based on what we knew at the time; we should have offered you protection without you having to suck up to Agent O'Connor. I want to apologize for that. My main reason for coming by to see you today was to let you know that we believe that any threat there might have been against you no longer exists."

"I saw where Dealin' Dave and his brother were arrested. Were they the threat?"

"They were arrested for a lot of things, but no. We believe their incompetence in handling illegal drugs contributed to deaths here and in Texas, but they weren't going after anyone. We also had our eye on Underwood, and we admit we should've acted sooner on that because he *was* a threat. How such a thug could become police chief in the first place would make an interesting story. Maybe that's something you should write about. He was a dangerous man, and he was your primary threat. Of course, his death ended that."

"So, everything is all cleaned up. No more crime." Tommy smiled.

"Yeah, that'd be great. But there are still some loose ends around here. One is Chuck Branson. We've been looking for him with help from the Air Force, but he's disappeared. We'll track him down, but we know he's left Oklahoma. Our last sighting was in Texas, near Houston. Based on information from the younger Harris brother, it appears Branson got involved because he saw an opportunity when Frank Martin left town. We believe he and the Harris brothers were amateurs who thought they could make a bunch of money. The prostitution was going okay for them, but they discovered a warehouse once owned by Martin containing a large amount of drugs. They thought they could handle that, too."

"They just stumbled across a warehouse full of drugs?" Tommy sounded skeptical.

"Our best guess is that Chuck knew about the warehouse. We think he was originally involved with Milton, the guy whose body was dumped at Tinker. We think Chuck was helping him bring the drugs in. We believe the warehouse was actually something he and Milton had, and Martin took it over. It looks like Chuck and Milton had a falling out, and that's when Milton went to Martin. Chuck was never involved with Martin, but he knew what was going on. We think Milton's body was dumped in Chuck's front yard as a warning for him not to get involved. Chuck moved it onto the base."

"You know this is on the record, right?"

"I'd prefer that you not quote me directly, but you can refer to this information and source it from a high-level FBI official." Swartz grinned. It reminded Tommy of a look Albright would give when he thought he was being clever.

"Well, that answers a lot of questions," Tommy said.

"Not all of them. This part I need to ask you not to repeat just yet. We believe there's someone else who was involved with Martin and connected with the chief. At one point we thought maybe Martin had something on the chief that forced him to help Martin. Now we think that wasn't how it worked. We think instead there's another person who somehow fits between those two guys. We believe it was that person who was controlling the chief, forcing him to help Martin. But at this point we don't have much to go on as to who that might be. So that's a loose end, but we do think any threat to you is now gone."

"I heard the Harris brothers were selling lots of cars in Texas. Someone told me it was maybe a couple hundred or thereabout over a short period of time. Do you know what that was about?"

"You have good sources." Swartz still looked friendly, but he was a little more cautious. "Can't give you all the details, but it was an effort to move the drugs from that warehouse to Texas. Selling the cars was a front for that, eventually sending them to Mexico. They packed the cars with drugs and delivered them. Once they heard about the drug-related deaths around here, all because they didn't know how to cut the stuff, they wanted to get rid of it, and fast. It actually wasn't a bad idea. It must've brought in a lot of cash. Which, by the way, we haven't been able to completely track down."

"Who would have thought that the nickname 'Dealin' Dave' would have actually meant 'Drug-Dealin' Dave?' Guess those guys are in some big trouble."

"Well, it still has to stand up in court. I saw their lawyer on television the other day, and I'd say the prosecutors will have their hands full. But that's not my job. I talked to Taylor the other day—he says you're one of the good guys. And not many people get a good rating from Taylor. If anything comes up where you need help again, just call me in Washington. I think O'Connor's being transferred to Wyoming next week, so he won't be around, anyway. Take care."

"You seem in a better mood."

"Yep. It's you, the FBI, and my agenda. Things are lookin' up." Tommy leaned over the table full of leftover pizza and gave Patsy a kiss. "Let's go home."

"Sounds like the best offer I've had today." Patsy had made up her mind at that moment that the next time Tommy asked her to marry him she was going to say yes, even if he was a baby.

OK Journal

My View—Tommy Jacks

The honest journalist's code says to tell it all and let the chips fall where they may. There's a reason for that, and it doesn't have a lot to do with the public's right to know. It's because that play generally works. It gets you the yards you need, if by "yards," you mean getting a tough point across.

But when the big hammer is about to come down, the right to know doesn't really figure into it. The right to know doesn't always cover the people about to feel the million-pound whack. The hammer is up, maybe a day or so away from the overhand delivery, and there's no way to know how many will get flattened under it.

Here's what we know: there was an insanely bad crime organization in our city, but for some reason the brains of the outfit pulled up stakes and left not long ago. That left a few spaces open, like a scuttled, festering house. And we all know what happened next: the rats came out of their holes and took over.

They nibbled their way into prostitution, buying up motels sleazy enough to suit them. They didn't need to recruit because they had a list to work from, which the king rat had packed away from a good source. We might find out who that was after the hammer hits.

But that's tough money, tougher than pushing heroin can get you. A guy can swear off visiting his favorite call girl for any number of self-preserving reasons, but smack does not let go. Period. The rats knew it and figured they could be the ones to take it to the streets.

Which, according to a source who happens to hold the hammer, they did. But that wasn't all there was to it. Maybe the rats didn't notice that heroin has fangs at one end and a stinger at the other, and that stinger comes out when you don't handle it right. The rats messed up bad, and littered our fair city with corpses.

One casualty was Sammy House, a formerly regular guy in his forties who looked like he'd passed his sixties without stopping by his fifties, until he took his last ride with a needle in an alley off Second Street. The coroner's report put him down as an overdose, but also made the point that what he'd used was strong enough to kill a grizzly. Another was Tina Duncan, whom some of you may remember. She was a blues singer with a promising future that the rats' poison denied her. The coroner said the smack he found inside her was stout enough to stop a freight train.

The rats—and no one's sure how many there are—felt the sting and panicked. They tried, with frantic abandon, to offload the junk. The details of that story might seem almost funny if it wasn't for all the shock and pain and excruciating death it left behind.

Now, here comes the hammer—not a moment too soon. 🐀

28
A SCENE FROM THE PAST

Tommy wasn't ready to get up. But the damn phone wouldn't stop. "Yeah, what?" He really was becoming Albright.

"Tommy? Vince. June just called me and said there was something going on at the Knight mansion. She told me to call you and let you know. I'm headed that way. You'll probably want to go out there."

"What *is* going on?"

"All she said was they heard on police radio that patrol cars and ambulances went to the senator's house. Sounds familiar, doesn't it?"

"Again? I'm on the way."

"What's going on?" Patsy wasn't completely awake. Lying in bed with her tousled hair, she looked fantastic, even first thing in the morning.

"That was Vince. The police are going to the Knight mansion for some reason, again. Don't know anything else yet. Once I find out anything and I can get to a phone, I'll call you at work. Or you could stay in bed, and I'll see you later." Tommy knelt down on the bed and gave her a gentle kiss.

"Well, that would be nice, but Uncle Larry is starting to grumble. I've got to be at work on time. So, give me a call when you can."

The sun wasn't up yet. It hadn't been that long ago he'd driven the same route on account of Janet Knight. That hadn't ended well. Tommy had a feeling this morning's events weren't going to wrap up happily either.

The police had set up barricades at each end of the street and weren't letting anyone get within two hundred feet of the house. Last time, TV people and reporters were all over the Knights' lawn before they could be herded off.

More police cars and emergency vehicles arrived as Tommy pulled near. The congestion of TV trucks and other vehicles was already creating problems. He had to park almost a quarter mile down the street.

Tommy spotted Vince. "No front row seats this time. Heard anything?"

Vince frowned at the crowds, just like the cops. "Nothing definite. Obviously, whatever it is has to do with the senator, but beyond that—" He shrugged. "Rumor has it that sometime last night or very early this morning someone heard gunshots coming from the house and called the cops. It's a little fuzzy after that. One guy here said he heard the cops came and Knight threatened them with a gun, so they backed off and called for reinforcements. They could see into some windows and said they saw a body—no idea who. Also, at some point the senator threatened to kill himself if they tried to get inside. I have no idea how much is factual, but it seems to fit what we're looking at."

The new police chief was moving among his men, giving encouragement and directions. It was hard to tell what they intended to do, if anything. They sure as hell didn't want a U.S. senator shooting himself because the cops broke into his house with TV cameras rolling.

"Hey there, handsome." Tracy gave Tommy her best movie-
star smile, although he saw a mom smile.

Tommy hugged her. "Is this one of your first in-field reports?"

"Yeah. My producer says this is 'TV gold.' The guy really
has no sense of what's going on with other people. So, I heard
the senator's refusing to come out and he's threatened to kill
himself?"

"That's more or less what Vince heard. Sure doesn't sound
like the Bruce Knight I met. Also, we heard there's a body on
the floor in the front room of the house."

"A body?"

"Yeah. I have a feeling we're witnessing a tragedy."

He and Tracy knew about tragedy. Both shuddered.

"Guess I better find my crew and get set up. We are going
'live' in just a little bit. The producer told me he wanted to
stretch this into the next scheduled show if we could. The man
doesn't seem to think about anything other than ratings. Well,
see ya later. Be careful."

"Is she really your mom?" Vince never knew when Tommy
was joking.

"Not yet."

Tommy thought the police looked like they were preparing
for a long standoff. Police cars were pulled up into the yard,
which created a wall officers could stay behind. That told him
they weren't prepared to force their way into the house. They
were going to wait the senator out.

"Hey, Tommy." Mike Sanders walked up to the barrier,
looking lost.

"Hello, Mike."

"Thanks for the story idea about Gail Collins. She was wonderful. I wrote up a piece, and your dad accepted it. They ran it this morning in the 'Life' section. Maybe not hard-hitting political stuff, but at least I got something in the paper."

"That's good, Mike. I'm sure you'll have a lot more." Tommy couldn't quite put his finger on why he was uncomfortable around Sanders. Maybe he was just too needy. In the distance, Tommy saw Agent Swartz in conversation with Chief Lawson, which struck him as unusual. A high-ranking Washington FBI agent at a local standoff? Swartz had already been in town when the situation came up, but it made Tommy wonder if, and how, the FBI was connected to Knight. Maybe it was just because he was a senator.

He headed back to where Vince was staked out. It looked like it might be a long wait before anything happened, but he had a powerful foreboding, something he'd had in the past, when things never turned out well. He found a spot to lean against a tree and closed his eyes.

The TV people in particular were getting restless. They preferred to cover action—flames, gunshots, rolling cars—anything that moved or blew up. Standing around wasn't good TV.

The street behind the barricade was so congested Tommy wasn't sure anyone could leave even if they wanted to. The cops might have a rebellion on their hands if something didn't happen soon. He looked up.

Now something was going on. Cops were moving around, at least. He saw some talking on police radios and walkie-talkies, maybe with Knight. What was the senator waiting for? A lieutenant from the police department came up to the barricades and shouted into the crowd.

"Is there a Tommy Jacks out here?"

His stomach did a quick backflip. "Yeah. Over here."

"Would you come with me, sir?" It wasn't a question, no matter how it was phrased. Tommy crossed the barricades and followed the officer toward the house, where Chief Lawson waited for him.

"Hello, Tommy. Glad you're here." He cleared his throat, ready to give particulars. "Senator Knight's in the house. He has a gun. And he's threatened to shoot if we try to go in. He's also threatened to kill himself. We're pretty sure he's shot someone. That person appears to be dead. It's a serious situation. We've been able to communicate with him over the last twenty minutes or so." Lawson fidgeted. "He's asked to speak to you."

"Me?"

"Yes. We don't know why. We're hoping he just wants to tell you something. Is there any reason he'd want to cause you any harm?"

A couple of possible answers flew through Tommy's head, but they were only wise-ass ones. He chose to go with simple and truthful. "No reason I know of. We only met once. I interviewed him some time ago. But there's nothing personal between us."

"Hello, Tommy."

Tommy turned to see Agent Swartz. "Hello, agent. Long ways from Washington."

"Yep. The chief told you Knight wants to see you. Before you decide whether to go in, you need to know that agents were following someone whom we suspect was the link between Martin and Underwood. They tailed him here late last night. There were shots fired inside the house. Our agents were preparing to go in when the local police showed up. The agents got hold of me. I didn't want to create a bigger mess, so I had them back off and let the local guys take charge. We still don't know why the guy we were watching came here. There could be a connection we don't know about. And it could put you at risk if for some reason you know something—maybe something you don't even know that you know."

"This might not seem reasonable, but I'm sure Knight wouldn't hurt me. I've met him, and I have no idea why he'd shoot anyone. But I'm not afraid of him at all." It wasn't bravado. Tommy really didn't fear Knight. He worried a little about being shot by an army of cops with itchy trigger fingers, but not by Knight.

The chief pulled Tommy aside to emphasize he wasn't being ordered to do what Knight asked, and the decision was entirely up to him. Still, even if Tommy thought Knight wouldn't hurt him, there was no way to know what he might do. "You do understand you're taking a risk—a very serious one?"

Tommy nodded. The chief got on the radio patched into the phone inside the house and told Knight that Tommy Jacks was ready to enter.

Tommy listened, suddenly having doubts. Maybe he shouldn't do this.

Tracy was at his shoulder, crying and shaking. "Tommy, you do not have to do this! These assholes should've never asked you to go in there. I won't let you. Do you understand me?"

Tommy wondered how she had gotten past the barricade and figured no one could have stopped her. He grabbed her and held on. "Don't worry. I think I know this man. He's in the middle of something very bad. But I don't believe he'd hurt me. I love you, Mom."

Tracy held on to him, refusing to let go. Tommy pulled away, gave her a kiss on the cheek, and whispered to her. "I'm one lucky kid."

He walked to the front door and paused. Then he went in.

29
HOME SWEET HOME

"Senator? It's Tommy Jacks. I'm coming in." He was nervous. He sure as hell didn't want to be killed because Knight might mistake him for a cop. Off the hallway he could see a body on the parlor floor. No question, it was a guy and he was dead. Blood spread in a dark pool on the wood floor.

He spoke up again. "Senator Knight. You asked to see me. I'm alone." He started to think about leaving. If Knight didn't want him there, he sure as hell didn't want to stay.

"Hello, Tommy." The senator stood on the staircase above the entry, speaking calmly. "Let's go into the kitchen." He led him to the back of the house. Tommy followed. "I made some coffee. Want some?

An absurd thought crossed Tommy's mind, that it could only have seemed weirder if the senator had said "tea." Wonderland in Oklahoma. "Sure, coffee would be great." He said no to sugar and cream. They took seats at a small breakfast nook, just like a normal coffee break.

"I shot Ralph Jenkins," Knight announced, still calm and civil, until he added with a slight snarl, "Should have killed that bastard years ago. I have no defense, really. He wasn't armed, just standing in my living room. And I shot him. I couldn't stand to listen to him for one more minute. So I killed him."

Knight sipped his coffee.

Tommy tried not to stare, feeling a chill and fighting down a shiver. "W-wasn't he your wife's doctor?"

"Yeah. The bastard weaseled himself into this house just to torment me." He sniffed. "I'm glad he's dead. I'm sorry Janet's dead. There aren't too many innocent people in my life, but she was one. She lived a very lonely life because she was so kind. I wish she was still around."

"What do you plan to do now?" Tommy wasn't sure how to talk to him. He didn't seem like the same man he'd met.

Knight seemed not to hear the question. "I'm going to tell you a story about some people," he began. "Some you've met, and some you know, and some maybe you don't. It will explain a lot about why things have happened the way they have. It'll definitely explain why I killed Ralph. What you do with that story will be up to you. I don't care. The first thing you should know is that I'm a homosexual." He looked up to read Tommy's reaction, which was only to keep his attention on him. "I didn't really understand that until I became an adult, living in Washington. I mean, I'd always known things were different with me. But I suppressed even my own thoughts, afraid of being found out as some kind of freak. For as long as I can remember, I'd been sad. I could fake it and act happy with people. But inside I felt sad. After I graduated from Yale, I was hired onto the staff of the senator from Connecticut. It was the best time of my life. I felt alive. I loved everything about the job—it was my future. I knew almost immediately that I wanted to be involved in politics. And I met the first person I ever loved—I still love him today. He was on the senator's staff, and the next few years were wonderful.

"The problem was, I wanted to run for Congress. Going back to Oklahoma to ask the good citizens for their vote, hand in hand with my boyfriend, wasn't going to work. I'd already built a reputation in Washington as one of the go-to people on almost everything to do with the Senate. I'd become visible. That's when I got a call from J.H. Gilmore. He wanted to see me. He was direct, wasted no time, just got right to the point. He said he thought I'd make a great senator, that the state needed someone young who knew how to make the Senate work for Oklahoma. I knew he meant I could make it work for *him*. He said that with his backing, and that of his paper, I could be the next U.S. senator from the state. I was floored. I'd been thinking about running for the House, but *senator!* It was unbelievable. He also said I couldn't be a queer and be a U.S. senator, too. I was fairly sure he really didn't care what I was. He said I'd have to get married, maybe have a kid, and then he could make me a senator. I knew it was a mistake. But I also knew right then that I'd do anything to be a senator. I moved back to Oklahoma and started working in the governor's office, all arranged by Gilmore. I was introduced to quite a few women—being set up for a marriage. And it happened. I met Janet, and we got married. Her father had business dealings with Gilmore, and I suspected she was bought, somehow. But she was unbelievably nice. The kindest person I've ever met. I tried to be normal as much as I could, and within an amazingly short time I was a U.S. senator. Of course, I wanted it all. I made one big mistake—I named my former boyfriend as my chief of staff. The attraction was still there, and I ended up spending more time with him than Janet. She found out," he sighed, "and came back here.

"The years passed, and we kind of adjusted. Janet and I weren't angry with each other, and we just fell into a rut of living apart—her here and me in Washington. The womanizing rumors came up because I would ask women to accompany me to certain events since Janet wasn't around. It wasn't intended as a cover story, but that's what it became.

"That should have been enough to worry about, but there was more. When I was a kid, I went to Central High, and Frank Martin and Ralph Jenkins were both in my graduating class. We weren't close, but I knew them, and we lived in the same neighborhood. I knew Martin had become a crook, and I guessed Ralph was involved with him. Frank was a thug, but he couldn't have organized anything, let alone a crime."

Tommy gulped. "Did you ever confront either of them?"

"Hell, no, Tommy." Knight almost chuckled. "Those guys were killers. I knew that as far back as high school. Frank, like I said, was just a thug, a brutal guy. But Ralph was some kind of crazy. He was evil in ways that made Frank look like an angel. I should've done something a long time ago, but I didn't. I think Ralph was running everything long before he became a doctor. He controlled Frank, and Frank took care of anyone who got in the way. I'm sure Ralph had some kind of control over Underwood, too. My guess is Underwood was being fed drugs by him.

"Ralph became a doctor. But he really only practiced one thing, and that was drug distribution. He only treated patients who needed or wanted painkillers. He made a fortune prescribing legal drugs. He got in trouble with the Federal Bureau of Narcotics once and came to see me in Washington. He was a scary kid, but he'd grown into a strange, crazy man. He told me he knew everything about my sex life, and that I'd better get the feds off of his back or my 'sickness' would be on page one of all the Oklahoma papers. I pulled every dirty political maneuver I could and got the feds to back off by promising my support for huge increases in their budgets." He grimaced. "I should've killed him then."

"Why would your wife choose him for a doctor?"

Knight frowned ruefully. "My wife, and maybe half of the town's bluebloods, liked the doctor's happy pills. He catered mostly to rich women. He went to every social gathering, donating lots of money to all the popular charities. They thought he was one of them. He wasn't. He gave them everything they wanted, and a lot more. He had hundreds of these women hooked on heroin, so he made even more money selling them that. I'm sure he was feeding it to Janet. She didn't know about our past, and of course, I wasn't around to help her."

"Did the doctor kill your wife?"

"Yes," he replied, looking up into Tommy's eyes. "That's what was behind it all. But I didn't know that until today. He showed up here about two in the morning. At first, I wouldn't let him in. The whole thing was so strange. He was pounding on the door. I got my gun and went downstairs. I would've been less scared if it had been a gang of robbers. He said if I didn't open the door, he'd tell the world all my secrets. I let him in.

Knight shook his head at the memory. "He was agitated. He said he was being followed—by the FBI, he thought. He wanted me to intervene on his behalf. He said he just needed a day, and after that, he'd be out of the country. I told him that was crazy. I had no way of contacting the FBI, and they sure wouldn't stop surveillance in an investigation on my account. He wouldn't listen. He just kept yelling at me. Then his expression changed, and he said he'd kill me, just like he killed my stupid wife. I asked him what he meant. He looked at me with cold eyes and told me what happened. He said she'd over-heard some of his conversations while she'd been high and he thought she was passed out—talk about drugs and his dealings with Frank. Janet knew Chief Underwood from the parties at his house just a few doors down from here. So she called him and told him she thought her doctor was involved in illegal drugs and other crimes. Underwood told Jenkins. He killed her with strychnine—told me that himself. I just reacted— didn't even think about it. I pulled out the gun and shot him." He set his jaw. "And I'm glad I did."

Tommy didn't want this to end badly. "You should give yourself up. There's a good chance you can get a lighter sentence because it was a crime of passion. He killed your wife and then bragged about it, for God's sake."

Knight smiled sadly. "Tommy," he sighed, "when you write your stories, don't make me out to be some kind of sad monster. My life hasn't been all bad. I wish I could've figured out a long time ago how to be different in this world without all the pain. But I'm not bitter. Life just didn't turn out the way I wanted. I think it's time for you to go. My advice isn't worth much, but it is this: you should always try to do the right thing."

Knight shook his hand and escorted him to the front door.

Tommy began to feel desperate. "Come out with me. What-ever will happen is better than what you're thinking of doing now. Please." He wanted to grab him and pull him outside and make him give himself up. He looked Knight in the eye.

"I couldn't stand to have all the dirt about me dragged out.

The humiliation would be far worse than death. Now, please—go." Knight gave him a slight shove, and Tommy stepped outside. He trotted toward Lawson.

"What did he say?"

"He told me his story. I think he might—" He looked up to see Tracy behind a patrol car. She was crying. He turned toward her but stopped short in reaction to a small explosion in the front of Knight's house. There were visible flames.

"What do we do now?" The question came from one of the captains to Chief Lawson.

"Get that fire crew over here, now." Lawson knew he'd get flak for not sending men inside, but he wasn't going to lose anyone for somebody who wanted to die anyway. At the same time, he couldn't stand by and watch a man burn to death. "I'm going in. Nobody else does anything until I give the okay."

They heard a gunshot. Everyone ducked instinctively, even if it was clear it came from inside and Knight likely wasn't aiming at anyone out there.

Lawson pushed open the front door slowly. He could see two bodies in the parlor. One was the senator's. He had shot himself through the head. He signaled to the fire department to move in. The firefighters dragged hoses and axes into the stately mansion.

The fire was quickly put out, and they discovered the propane bottle used for the explosion. Tommy thought maybe burning the house was somehow symbolic for Knight, erasing the pain of a troubled life.

Tommy told Knight's story to Chief Lawson and the FBI. He

was a journalist, but he could not bring himself to spill everything he had learned. Even if it was his job to chronicle the joys and misery of life, this story felt like a confession, too private and personal. He still didn't know what he thought about the complicated Senator Knight, but he knew he couldn't be the one to "drag out the dirt" about a man who'd suffered so much. Knight could've lessened that pain but was unable to walk away from his addiction to power. He paid a steep price for fame and fortune. He'd wanted it all but had given up so much, and eventually lost everything.

30

BRIDES AND FAIRY TALES

It was a gloomy day in Oklahoma, overcast with brief showers. Perfect for a wedding. Everyone was supposed to meet at the courthouse at two. Patsy and Tommy were there. But, no bride or groom.

"Okay, Miss Patsy, here's your chance. We can get married right here, in this very courthouse. Great idea?"

"Stupid idea. We have to get a license first, and we need a blood test. We can't just walk in and tell them to marry us on the spot."

"Government control has gotten out of hand. Next thing, they'll be regulating bathroom breaks at ball games."

Patsy looked at her future husband in an odd way, as if wondering whether she was making a mistake. No, maybe not. It could be better that he was slightly crazy.

"Hi, there. Sorry we're late. Last-minute jitters or something. Anyway, we're here now. Let's go in and get started." Ray Jacks was all smiles. Tracy looked worried.

Patsy sensed it. "Tracy, you're so beautiful. That dress is amazing. You okay?"

"You guys go in. I want to talk to Patsy just a minute." Tracy steered her to a spot away from the door. "I'm so nervous, I think I might throw up."

Patsy wasn't sure she understood. Tracy and Ray weren't exactly kids, and nobody was forcing this to happen. "Why so nervous?" Patsy used her "I might be talking to a crazy person" voice.

"Ray's been married three times. I've never been, not once. I'm just not sure." Tracy wrung her hands.

Patsy's image of Tracy was of a no-nonsense woman who could handle anything. To see her this way was disturbing and charming at the same time. *I guess anyone can get nervous about this kind of commitment.* "If you want to cancel, I'll take you home or wherever you want to go. We can leave right now. They'll figure it out. You don't have to do this. Let's just go."

Tracy looked startled. "No." She took a deep breath. "No, this is silly. I love Ray. He's a good man, and my god, we've been living together. I know who he is, his faults, weaknesses— all the bad stuff, I already know. What's wrong with me?"

"Would you rather have a bigger wedding?"

"Oh goodness, no. I was the one who insisted on making it as simple as possible. I know I'd bail out of a big wedding. I'm just a coward. I don't want to be hurt. It's Ray, but it's also Tommy. I know he jokes about me being his mom, but now I really will be. Can I do that?"

"Of course you can. All of you have shared so much pain, it's time to share some joy.

Tracy looked at Patsy for a long time. "You're a sweet girl. I hope you and Tommy make it." They hugged and Tracy fixed her hair. "Let's go."

When they entered, Ray rushed up. "Is everything okay?"

"Yep, just great."

They were married on a gloomy day in the Oklahoma

County Courthouse by a clerk named Betty, who thought Tracy looked just like someone on TV, and cried through much of the short ceremony.

"You know; Tracy was really nervous." Patsy sat close to Tommy in his ratty old Ford.

"Yeah, I saw that. I was afraid she might back out. I mean, it would've been okay. My dad has a lousy track record. Anybody would've understood," Tommy lied. Of course, he would have broken down if she'd backed out.

"Well, I think they made Betty's day. She told me after the ceremony she was sure Tracy was a movie star, but she couldn't think of her name."

"I'm going to stop up here at that newsstand and get some newspapers."

Patsy shook her head with a knowing grin. "Why don't you just call him?"

"Yeah," he sighed. "Of course, he didn't give me his number."

"Call information. I know it's a big town, but he might have a listed number. There's a phone booth, right there."

Tommy looked at Patsy. "Thanks."

He called information and gave them the town and name. They came back in seconds and gave him a number. He wrote it down on an old piece of paper out of his pocket, then looked at the number, hesitating. Why hadn't Albright called him? He shoved the paper back into his pocket.

"Did you get hold of him?"

"Nah, they didn't have a number."

❀

"I know you changed your mind today. Why did you go through with it?"

"For the honeymoon sex." She giggled like a little girl.

"That's okay by me. But I know it's not why. Tell me, why did we get married today when you weren't sure?"

"I love you, Ray. I love Tommy, and I'm starting to love Patsy. It's a family. For most of my life I only had my father. He was my entire family. When he was killed, I almost died. I'd never felt that kind of loss. At first, I was so angry that all I wanted was to attack someone. But in just a few short hours I was devastated. I completely fell apart. It took days for me to just stand up, much less function. One of the reasons I was able to recover was you. Yes—you." She sat up. "I knew we connected, but I also knew something about your history. I told myself that I wasn't being rational, that you were too risky. I can't really explain it, but I thought we could be a couple, that you'd comfort me in my loss and everything would be good again, someday. Probably just a silly fantasy to distract me from the reality of my father's death, but it gave me hope. Then you went to jail. I can't tell you what that did to me—and we weren't even dating. We hardly knew each other. You had no idea how I felt, but in my mind, you were going to help me get back to some kind of normal, and then you were gone. I hated you, and I hated life. I functioned, but that was about it. And then, years later, the tragedy with Judy and Tommy happened. I thought I would go mad, that I could never have a normal life. Now here we are, almost normal. I panicked—I can't lose you or Tommy. I got over it once, but I can't do it again. I almost backed out because I was terrified of being hurt that bad again."

Ray wasn't sure what to say, so he held her, for a long time. "Life shouldn't be so hard," she said at last.

"No, it shouldn't be." Ray looked at Tracy, so she could see the love in his eyes. "We need to find our fairy-tale ending."

ABOUT THE AUTHORS

Ted Clifton has written mystery novels which feature the settings of New Mexico and Oklahoma, places where Ted spent considerable time. One of his books, *The Bootlegger's Legacy*, won the IBPA Benjamin Franklin award and the CIPA EVVY award. Today Ted and his wife reside in Denver, Colorado, after many years living in the New Mexico desert.

Once a month, Ted sends his readers a newsletter with a little of everything in it: southwest US culture, be it art, recipes, or local sights; his thoughts on writing and reading; book recommendations; updates on his current writing projects; and from time-to-time a short story.

To sign up, visit TedClifton.com and either wait for the pop-up window, or scroll to the bottom of the page. Everybody who signs up receives a mystery gift, with Ted's compliments. You can also learn more about Ted and his latest books by visiting TedClifton.com or emailing him at ask@tedclifton.com.

Stanley Nelson lives in Oklahoma, and works for what is presently the only book publisher staffed and operated by a Native American tribe. His background includes several years in newspapers as an editor and columnist. He edits and supplies text for several of the publisher's titles, and authored *Toli: Chickasaw Stickball Then and Now*, winner of an IBPA 2017 Gold Medal for Regional Non-Fiction.

BOOKS BY TED CLIFTON

Available from popular booksellers.

MURDER SO STRANGE

Muckraker Mystery #2

In an exclusive residential neighborhood, a U.S. Senator's wife has died. Tommy Jacks and his fellow journalists don't believe the police chief's story blaming it on natural causes. It has the smell of a crime. So begins a new journey set in the 1960s involving numerous dead bodies, high-tension political intrigue, police corruption, the drug underworld and unsavory hidden pasts. Tommy has a lot to write about in his My View political column.

Only in his second year as a political columnist, he finds new romance and emotional healing among a chaotic mixture of characters, from his new mother and his recently out-of-jail father to his acerbic journalistic mentor and antagonist and a foul-mouthed lawyer of questionable ethics, all wrapped inside the saga of two competing daily newspapers still at war.

Lurking in the shadows is the powerful and corrupt police chief, who seems to think it might be best if Mister Jacks, even so young, was dead.

Murder So Strange continues the 1960s saga of Tommy Jacks: Muckraker.

MURDER SO FINAL

Muckraker Mystery #3

Tommy Jacks, reporter, encounters new love and old threats while covering one of the most brutal U.S. Senate races in history. With a massive oil fire threatening the city of Tulsa, three candidates face off: a ruthless oil baron, an idealist college professor, and a reverend running under the God Party. When the race suddenly turns deadly, the winner may be the last man standing.

The final book in the Muckraker trilogy, Murder So Final brings to a close the stories of Louongo, Albright, Robbie Gilmore, Tracy and Ray Jacks, and Tommy himself.

DOG GONE LIES

Pacheco & Chino Mysteries #1

Sheriff Ray Pacheco returns from his introduction in The Bootlegger's Legacy to start a new chapter as a private investigator, along with his partners: Tyee Chino, often-drunk Apache fishing guide, and Big Jack, bait shop owner and philosopher.

The trio are pulled into a mystery immediately when an abandoned show dog appears at Ray's cabin and the dog's owner is reported missing. Ray and his team pursue leads that bring them into confrontations with the local sheriff, the mayor, and the FBI, while in the meantime two bodies are found—neither of which is the missing woman.

SKY HIGH STAKES

Pacheco & Chino Mysteries #2

Tired of spending his days fishing, Ray Pacheco takes on his second assignment with his partner Tyee Chino when the state Attorney General asks them to find out just what the hell is going on in Ruidoso, New Mexico. With the town's sheriff in the hospital with a mysterious illness, acting sheriff Martin Marino is running rough-shod over everyone around him.

What seems like a simple assignment becomes more complicated when Marino is found dead, shot at close range while sitting in his patrol car on Main Street. The suspects include most of the town, from Dick Franklin, manager of Ruidoso Downs racetrack, to bar owner Tito Annoya, to members of the local law enforcement.

At the same time, Ray has an uneasy feeling that the AG is withholding critical details about what exactly is going on in Ruidoso—and why the state was so slow to respond.

It all comes to a surprising conclusion with the involvement of a Spanish princess, a drug lord gone mad, and a few other lowlifes . . . and leaves Ray wondering if maybe fishing wasn't so boring after all.

FOUR CORNERS WAR

Pacheco & Chino Mysteries #3

Rejoin Ray Pacheco and Tyee Chino in their latest adventure unraveling a maze of misdeeds involving wealth, power, political corruption and Navajo warriors.

Farmington, New Mexico, located in the Four Corners area

where four states meet, is about to experience a level of crime and mayhem never seen before. The local sheriff has abandoned his post and taken old military equipment, including a tank, off to Colorado to prepare for the beginning of the end. Left behind is the body of his wife, who was having an affair with the richest man in town.

Money, sex and all known sins come into play in a small-town drama that will take Pacheco and Chino into a conflict that will involve many of the good citizens of Farmington and the nearby Navajo Nation.

SANTA FE MOJO
Vincent Malone Book 1

Vincent Malone was once a hot-shot Dallas attorney, but booze and bad judgement brought that and his marriage to an abrupt end. Battling gout and barely paying the bills as a legal investigator, Malone's unreliability costs him his last client.

Heading south with no idea of what the future may hold, Malone takes a know-nothing job as a shuttle driver for a B&B in Santa Fe, where he meets the clients of a big-time LA sports agent. Gathered to celebrate their success, things go sour quickly when missing millions, sexual entanglements, and personal histories lead to murder.

Malone finds himself in the middle of a major murder case with the lead detective giving him the evil eye. Malone teams up with an aging gun-slinger attorney to find the real killer and clear an innocent man.

BLUE FLOWER RED THORNS

Vincent Malone Book 2

Vincent Malone, hot-shot attorney turned shuttle driver, finds himself in the middle of another murder case.

The international contemporary art scene has come to Santa Fe, New Mexico, and brought plenty of ego, feuds, and sexual entanglements along with it. Vincent's employer, the Blue Door inn, is hosting a big artist for her U.S. debut and nothing is going smoothly. The artist and gallery owner are threatening each other, and before long there is one dead body and plenty of suspects.

Malone dusts off his private investigator skills to solve this tangled mystery with an unusual cast of characters, plenty of false leads, and a surprise ending following many twists and turns.

FICTION NO MORE

Vincent Malone Book 3

A mystery author staying at the Blue Door Inn claims she is being followed. Vincent Malone volunteers to find out what is going on, and things quickly get complicated.

The author's first book is about a murder that took place forty years in the past, but the details are suspiciously specific. The victim's adult son would like to know how the author came by this information. Soon, a bullying sheriff and a wayward priest are involved, along with a priceless—and stolen—collection of Pueblo Indian artifacts.

When the situation turns deadly, Malone must find out

who committed the murder, and why. Past misdeeds long buried will come to light, and fiction will be separated from fact, as Malone pursues the truth.

THE BOOTLEGGER'S LEGACY

Prequel to the Pacheco & Chino mystery series.

When an old-time bootlegger dies and leaves his son Mike a cryptic letter hinting at millions in hidden cash, Mike and his friend Joe embark on a journey that takes them through three states and 50 years of history. What they find goes beyond money and transforms them both.

This is an action-packed adventure story that partially takes place in the early 1950s. It all starts with a key, embossed with the letters CB, and a cryptic reference to Deep Deuce, a neighborhood once filled with hot jazz and gangs of bootleggers. Out of those threads is woven a tapestry of history, romance, drama, and mystery; connecting two generations and two families in the adventure of a lifetime.

Winner of the IBPA Benjamin Frankling Digital Awards (2016 Silver Honoree).

> "The Bootlegger's Legacy takes the reader on a wild ride through Oklahoma's bootlegging history. It makes for a wonderful escape into a fascinating, dangerous, and strange world filled with characters your mother warned you about. Most readers will only ever interact with these types in make believe, but while the ride lasts it's a rollicking good time."
>
> —*Self-Publishing Review, 4 Stars*

"Although the mystery elements in this novel are certainly engaging enough to keep readers turning pages, it's Clifton's superb character development that makes this story a transformative journey of self-discovery. The noteworthy narrative also includes vivid backdrops, brisk pacing, and a meticulously researched, historically accurate account of the Prohibition era in Oklahoma and Texas. A tale with an authentic, immersive setting, inhabited by well-developed, endearing characters."

—*Kirkus Reviews*